FAMILY AFFAIRS

A Swamp Yankee Mystery

BOOK FOUR

JAMES Y. BARTLETT

Copyright © 2023 by James Y. Bartlett

For information contact;

Yeoman House Books
10 Old Bulgarmarsh Road
Tiverton, RI 02878

www.jamesybartlett.com

Cover design by Todd Fitz of Fuel Media

Cover image: "Creative Commons 166a.33rdNPOM.USC.WDC. 15May2014(State Police Officer)" by Elvert Barnes is licensed under CC BY-SA 2.0. The original image has been modified.

ISBN: 978-1-7363930-9-3

First Edition: March 2023

Second Edition April 2026

10 9 8 7 6 5 4 3 2 1

All happy families are alike;
each unhappy family is unhappy in its own way.

--Leo Tolstoy, Anna Karenina

CHAPTER 1

I WAS ENJOYING the warm sun of an early October afternoon on the deck behind my house. Here in southern New England, we have more than our fair share of crappy weather. Enough to make many of us cranky much of the year. From December through March, and sometimes a little more on either end, we are subject to blizzards, ice storms, or cold sideways rain. Sure, we all have our L.L. Bean flannel shirts and fuzzy-flap lumberjack's hats and lined gloves and mittens and thick woolly socks … but winter in New England can be cold and damp and unpleasant.

March and April are the heartbreakers: there are hints that the long cold winter of our discontent has passed, but those brief hints are followed by more cold, more snow, more freezing. July and August can be scorchers, with high heat and humidity making summer life entirely unpleasant; and September can be a reverse heartbreaker, with hints of cool fall followed by another week in the 90s.

But October's weather, which sometimes lasts well into early November … now those are the weeks we love around here. That big ole ocean out there finally gets to its peak warm temperatures in August and holds onto that warmth until the first freeze. Warm ocean means warm air. So even as the days get shorter and the trees start to turn colors, October is usually close to perfect: warm sunny days and clear cool nights good for sleeping with the windows open and a light blanket on the bed. Unless a hurricane blows up from the tropics, we get perfect football weather. Or late-season baseball weather. Or for the kids in high school, great weather for soccer and cross-country. Also great weather for golf, tennis, boating, fishing, cleaning up the garden, washing the car, doing a little painting or fix-up around the house. Don't need the heater, don't need the air conditioning. Just 30 or so perfect weather days.

So I was enjoying one, reading a book, sipping from a tall glass of iced tea and occasionally looking out at the Rockies, that collection of rocky islets and barnacle-covered boulders that lay just offshore of my beachfront home, around and through which the tides flowed happily, sparkles from the golden sun dancing atop the waves as they lapped on the rocky surfaces and the beach.

I had given myself permission to take the afternoon off. I'm retired, remember? My part-time private eye business had surprisingly been keeping me pretty busy over the last few months. When I helped my son, the current chief of police in our little Rhode Island town of Little Penwick, solve a 30-year-old cold case a few months back, I got my name in the paper. And that helped get the phone to ring. I now had three local law firms, one here in town and two more over in Newport, put me on the list of people they called for help to track down skip tracers, research insurance claimants and even do a couple of domestics. Those aren't my favorites — the world is an unhappy enough place without me having to follow around one spouse or another to see if they're doing the afternoon delight thing, and with whom — but the money is pretty good.

And in between times, I had been helping my son Gus build his new house, over near Niwosauket Pond. We had the foundations poured, the first-floor studs were up and work was moving right along. Right on schedule for the January appearance of Gus and Maggie's first child, a blessed event we were all looking forward to. Of course, Gus was pretty busy being chief of police, even though Little Penwick is not exactly a town rife with crime. I should know, since I had been chief of the department for twenty-six years, plus another ten as an officer on the force. While we occasionally had some bad crimes here — that 30-year-old Donna Dixon case had been one — most of the time life was pretty calm around here.

Siggi, my significant other, was working this afternoon at Dr. Harley's pediatrician office near the village green, and she'd be over later for dinner. So I was chilling out on the deck, working my way slowly through Howard Zinn's A People's History of the United States. I'd never gotten around to reading it before — it certainly wasn't on the reading list of the police academy when I went through there fifty years ago. But I thought it was about time, since Zinn was one of the first of the latter-day historians who decided to take an entirely new look at our historical record, this time through the lens of his classest, Marxist, anti-capitalist beliefs. You could draw a straight line between Zinn and people like Ibram X. Kendi and Nicole Hannah-Jones and the Critical Race theorists that had so many people's panties wadded up these days.

I was following the part where Zinn was writing about the prehistoric Moundbuilders of the Ohio River valley and their egalitarian culture, when I caught a movement in the corner of my eye at the fence on the far end of the deck. I glanced up and saw the head of a boy. He looked to be about twelve or thirteen or so. Tousled hair, brownish red, with a scattering of freckles across the forehead. He was staring at me over the top of the wall.

"Hey, there," I said. "Beautiful day, isn't it?"

His eyes widened slightly, but he said nothing.

"School out already?" I kept going. Mentally, I was trying to place him, but wasn't having any luck. I knew all my neighbors, and I didn't have that many, but couldn't think of any family nearby that had a pre-teen boy like this.

He didn't respond to that, either.

"You want some ice tea?" I said next. "I can scare you up a glass."

He smiled and shook his head. I wanted to pump my fist —Breakthrough! A reaction!!— but didn't.

"You're that cop," the boy said. His small dark eyes were fixated on me.

"Guilty," I said, putting the flap of the dust jacket in place and closing my book. "But I'm a retired cop now. Used to be the chief around here. Now my son is the chief." I looked up at him. He seemed to be following all that. "You need a cop, son?"

He blinked twice and then his head disappeared. When it didn't immediately reappear above my fence, I stood up and wandered over to the end of the deck. Looking back up towards the street from which my crushed oyster-shell driveway came down, I saw the kid climbing onto a bike, one of those with all-terrain dirt-bike tires and raked back handlebars.

"Hey!" I called out to him. He stopped, now athwart his bike and looked back at me. "You want to come back anytime, just come round the walkway between the house and the garage," I said. "I'm here most of the time. Knock on the back door. I'll keep the pitcher of tea cold for ya."

He smiled again, gave me a half-wave of acknowledgment, and rode away.

I DIDN'T THINK much about the boy after that. I went back to my book and chugged slowly through a couple more chapters. By then, my tea was gone and the sun was sinking fast into Aquidneck Island off to the west. I checked my watch and saw it was almost 4:30, so I figured I'd better get started on dinner. Siggi would be home soon, and after a long day chasing kids around the pediatrician's office, she'd be beat. I was planning some braised pork chops, along with some slaw from the head of red cabbage I had. Plus, I had a nice bottle of red from the local Sakonnet Vineyards in town, a blend of cab franc, merlot, and lemberger, a grape that did well in our local terroir.

I went inside, got the chops out of the fridge, washed and dried them and hit them with a lot of salt and pepper. I seared them with a little oil in a hot skillet and then put the chops and the skillet in a medium oven to roast away slowly for an hour or so. Then I got the cabbage out along with my big knife and was about to commence chopping when I heard Siggi's car pull down the driveway.

I stopped with the cabbage and opened the bottle of red. It needed to breathe a little and Siggi, after a quick shower and change of clothes, would be very ready for a glass.

Siggi didn't come in right away, which I thought idly was a little weird, but then she did. I turned to greet her with a smile, and saw the look on her face. The smile disappeared.

"Julius?" she said, voice wavering a bit. Her eyes were searching mine. Something was not right.

"What's the matter?" I asked.

"There's some men here," she said, "And ...'

Two large men came in the back door behind her. One was dressed in civilian clothes, a shirt and tie under a navy blue windbreaker jacket. The other was dressed in the full monty uniform of the Rhode Island State Police. He wore a gray jacket with flapped front pockets, a gray shirt and a dark grey tie, those absurd red-striped grey paints flared at the top that narrow down to stuff into the calf-height polished brown boots with a row of brass buttons down the front, and the round khaki-colored Stetson hats with the leather band and a nicely defined scoop depression in the front. Like a dimple in one's cheek. And, of course, the brown leather harness around the waist with the narrow leather strap up across the chest. It's a uniform that never fails to look great in a Fourth of July parade, but one in which I cannot imagine doing any kind of law enforcement in. At least, without falling down.

"Julius Haddock?" said the one dressed like a human being. The full monty trooper carefully edged Siggi out of the way. Just in case I went for my gun and started shooting. Which would be hard, since my firearm was in its holster hanging in my bedroom closet.

"Who wants to know?" I said. I know, a simple 'yes' would have sufficed. But they had just come crashing uninvited into my home, and I was not in the mood to be cooperative.

"We'd like you to come with us, please," the windbreaker guy said.

"Sure," I said. "Soon as you tell me why, where and what the hell is going on."

"We'd like you to answer some questions," windbreaker guy said. "Over at the Portsmouth barracks."

"Answer questions about what?"

"You are a person of interest," he said.

"I'm glad somebody finally noticed," I said. "But what case am I supposedly involved in?"

"Preston Knox," he said. Both of them gave me the stink eye. Waiting for me to begin shrieking and wailing 'I didn't do it, you got the wrong guy!'

Instead, I said "The attorney general? What about him?"

"He was murdered this morning," windbreaker guy said. "We want to talk to you about that."

Siggi caught her breath and her hand went involuntarily up to her throat. Both the staties noticed.

I had been holding the corkscrew and cork all this time. Now, I carefully laid it down on the counter. I looked at Siggi.

"Call Gus," I said. "Tell him to meet me over at the Portsmouth barracks."

She nodded, most of the color drained from her face. I smiled at her, reassuringly.

"No worries," I said. "Just call Gus. Oh, and the pork chops are in the oven. Take them out in about forty minutes." She nodded again. She was still ashen faced. I turned to the staties.

"OK," I said, "Let's go."

CHAPTER 2

I RODE IN the back of their squad car, but they didn't cuff me first. Professional courtesy, probably. It wasn't a long drive over to the Portsmouth barracks, located in a Georgian-style brick building off East Main Road on Aquidneck Island, across the river from Little Penwick.

They took me upstairs to a windowless interview room with a metal table in the middle of the room, and two chairs on each side. I sat down facing the door. Windbreaker and the Full Monty left me there by myself to stew. So far, usual interview procedure. If I had been considered a dangerous criminal, I would have been shackled to the metal table, which in turn was bolted to the floor. Instead, I rubbed my free wrists and tried not to think about the eight months I had spent in jail the year before, thanks in large part to the corrupt work of Preston Knox, the attorney general of the state of Rhode Island. The *late* attorney general.

That's why the staties wanted to talk to me. I was a fairly high-profile former case on the AG's docket, and my case had not turned out well for him. Knox had been protecting the shadowy group that owned a string of strip clubs in Providence and around New England, and God knows what other criminal enterprises, in return for lots of campaign donations. One associate of that group, which we used to call the Mafia before that became politically incorrect, was an old guy who lived in my town, Little Penwick. And that old guy, Angelo Ferro, had in turn worked closely with a young woman, first imported to work in those strip clubs, who had instead proposed new ways of bringing in 'talent.' Strippers and whores. From both domestic and international locations. She had worked out a way to smuggle the foreign sex workers into the country right through Little Penwick.

Well, one cold winter's night a year ago, that old guy had disappeared. Along with his 40-foot fishing vessel. Never to be seen again. Naturally, as chief of police, I had started an investigation into that disappearance. In Little Penwick, our people usually don't spontaneously disappear, so we tried to find out where he had gone.

The Committee, the wizened old criminals who ran the strip club operation, told Knox to put the kibosh on my investigation. Not being one of the smarter cards in the deck, Knox called in some chits with some old judge and had me sent off to the ACI —the Adult Correctional Institution—on some drummed-up payola scheme that everyone knew was crap. They say Rhode Island is the 'I know a guy' state, and Preston Knox knew the guys he could call on to send me away.

In turn, I had contacted my son, then a Lieutenant in the Army Rangers on assignment in Falluja, and he had quickly resigned and came home. Because he had already served five years as a patrolman in town, the town council named him to replace me as chief of police in Little Penwick. Yes, I, too, had called in some chits to get that deal done. I had quite a few chits in the bank after twenty-siz years as chief. I knew a few guys, too. So Gus came home, was named chief, and took over the investigation into the Angelo Ferro disappearance case, learned about the Glitter Girl who ran the human smuggling operation and put an end to it.

And I came home, case dismissed. Older, wiser, grayer and semi-retired. I was happy to let Gus take over the family business at the department. It's in good and capable hands. Siggi was happy I wasn't sleeping at the ACI with murderers and rapists. I sorta was, too. And I activated my state-issued private investigator's license, which gave me something to do with my days. I helped solve that 30-year-old cold case, for a start.

Still, I could understand why the state police were interested in talking to me about the murder of Preston Knox. I had been unfairly prosecuted, after all. I had a grudge. I wanted revenge. And they were right: if I could have figured out a way to do it without being caught, I almost certainly would have put a couple of caps into Preston's noggin. There are always a few people in the world who deserve not to be here. He was one of them.

But I didn't do it. Not sorry someone did. But it wasn't me.

The door opened and two men came into the room. These two were both dressed in business attire, which is good, because I was tired of looking at the para-military trooper. One of the two was a guy I knew, Davis Ruggerio, who was about my age. He was chief of detectives in the Major Crime bureau of the state police. He was a heavy set man with receding gray hair and a round face which matched a body that had seen just a bit too much *pasta puttanesca*. But he had quick little eyes that took in everything and sent it up to the computer in his head for storage and future processing. We had encountered each other a few times over the decades I was chief in Little Penwick. I had no beef with him. He was a cop's cop. So was I, of course, but today, in this little airless room, we were on opposite sides in every sense.

The other guy was a tall slender black man I did not know. He was carrying the file folder, so I figured him to be the junior officer.

"Hello, Julius," Davis said, nodding at me as he sat down. "Thanks for coming in."

"Did I have a choice?" I asked.

Davis ignored me. "This is Detective Jonah Allen, assigned to the Major Crimes unit."

I reached my hand across the table. Allen looked surprised, but he eventually gave me a brief shake. I wanted to make sure he didn't see me as a perp, right from the get-go. I was a cop. An ex-cop, but one never leaves the brotherhood. I wanted to get that out there.

"This interview, with former Little Penwick chief of police Julius C. Haddock, is being recorded," Davis intoned for the record and nodded at a black box on a shelf on the wall to my left. I glanced up to the corner of the room and saw the unblinking eye of a digital camera.

"You gonna read me my rights?" I said, smiling at Davis.

"Do I need to?" he replied.

I shrugged. "Your rodeo," I said.

"I take it you've heard the news," Davis said. "About the attorney general."

"First I heard of it was when your goons ... I mean, the troopers ... arrived at my home an hour or so ago," I said. "What happened?"

"An unknown assailant entered the home of Preston Knox in Barrington this morning, sometime between seven-thirty and ten o'clock," Jonah Allen said. "He was beaten to death."

"With what?" I said.

Allen shook his head. He wasn't going to tell me. Yet.

"Where was his bodyguard?" I said. "What was that guy's name ... John or Jack or something?"

"John Richardson," Davis Ruggerio said. "Plainclothes trooper assigned to the government security detail. He was Preston's driver and day watch minder. He found the body when he reported to the attorney general's residence at ten. You knew him?"

I nodded. "I met him once or twice with Preston earlier this year," I said.

"When and where did you meet with the attorney general?" Ruggerio asked the question in his best stentorian police officer tone of voice.

"I caught a speech Preston made in Newport last spring," I said. "Richardson was with him. I spoke to both of them at that event. And Preston came down to Little Penwick to make a speech at our town picnic on Memorial Day. I believe John was there, too. I did not speak with either of them on that occasion."

"I understand that Mr. Knox's appearance in Little Penwick was not well received," Ruggerio said.

"In Little Penwick? No, he was pretty much booed out of town."

"Why is that?"

I shrugged. "Could be because he was a crap politician who said nothing the people wanted to hear," I said. "Or maybe because he had arrested one of the town's police chiefs — that'd be me — and then harassed the next one, which would be my son Gus. But that's all just speculation on my part. I don't know why the good people of Little Penwick didn't like Knox. I don't do politics. I'm a cop."

"Preston Knox was the Democratic candidate for Governor," Ruggerio said. "The election is not quite a month away. You know that, don't you?"

"Yeah," I said, "I guess I'd heard that. Hey! I wonder if his Republican opponent snuck in his house and beat him to death? Have you thought of that? It's about the only way a Republican has a chance in this state."

"Our investigation is proceeding in several directions," Ruggerio said. "Which is why we wanted you to come and and speak with us tonight."

"And here I am," I said.

"You didn't like the attorney general, did you?" The question came from Jonah Allen. I couldn't tell yet if he was gonna be the bad cop to Davis Ruggerio's good one. But they'd done everything so far according to the book, so I figured that was coming, in whatever configuration.

"No," I said, "I did not."

"Why is that?"

"Because, to cover up his own corruption and malfeasance, he had a Superior Court judge toss me into the ACI so he could protect the criminals running a human trafficking ring through my town. He used his long personal connections with another judge to impede the investigation into that trafficking ring run by my son, the new chief of police in Little Penwick." Both of the staties were listening with stone faces, giving nothing away.

"And," I said, "I believe that if you do a little digging, you will likely find some cases of sexual harassment or assault from some of the women he employed in his 'harem' at the attorney general's office. He has a history of such actions throughout his life, going back to his college days at Dartmouth." I paused, thinking. "So, no, I did not think Preston Knox was an honorable man. Or a good public servant."

"Did you hate him enough to kill him?" Jonah Allen asked the sixty thousand dollar question. I guess he was the bad cop.

"Sure," I said. "I hate all the politicians who cheat and steal and abuse other people for their own gain."

"So you admit you killed Preston Knox this morning?"

I laughed. "No, detective," I said. "I admit I hated the guy. But I was nowhere near Barrington this morning. Don't think I've been through that town in more than a year. Sorry."

"I take it you have some alibis or witnesses that can prove that?" Davis Ruggerio, the good cop, jumped back in.

"Why yes," I said. "I do."

The door to the interview room opened and my son walked in.

"Chief of Police Gus Haddock of Little Penwick has entered the interview room," Davis Ruggerio said in his policeman's official voice.

"And Chief of pPolice Gus Haddock is taking this gentleman home with him," Gus said, pointing at me. "The senior Mr. Haddock and I had coffee and a scone together this morning at approximately eight-thirty at the Commons Cup, an establishment on the town green in Little Penwick. I don't remember how many other citizens were also there this morning, but if you insist, I can get the proprietor, Ms. Betty Billingsly, to swear an affadavit listing all those she recalls were in her coffee shop today. We were at the Commons Cup for almost an hour. Mr. Haddock's partner, Ms. Siggi Andersen was with Mr. Haddock before that. There is no way Mr. Haddock could have traveled from Little Penwick all the way up to Barrington and back within the time frame of the events of this morning."

"He could have hired someone to do it," Jonah Allen said, playing the bad cop role to the bitter end.

Gus looked at him sadly. "You had better have pretty good proof of that, sir," he said. "And I mean eight-by-ten glossies, video tape or a signed and sworn statement by an eye witness."

"Thank you, Chief Haddock," Ruggerio said, sitting back in his chair. "This interview is concluded at ..." He glanced at his watch. "…seven forty-two p.m. Julius Haddock is released without further instance, although we may ask him to return for an additional interview if the investigation indicates a need for such."

He reached up to the box on the shelf and clicked the machine off. I stopped myself from giving a little wink and a wave to the camera in the corner.

The door to the interview room opened again and two more people walked into the room, which was becoming smaller by the second. When I saw who it was, I sat up a little straighter.

Cara Romero was our governor, at least for another couple of months. She had been in office the last eight years and had done a pretty good job. The state hadn't gone broke, the budget was within hailing distance of being balanced, and most agencies in the state were working with a reasonable degree of efficiency. Except the Department of Motor Vehicles, of course. You would think the DMV, which is annually the most vilified agency in state government, could get its act together and be able to process a renewed driver's license or a car registration transaction in less than three hours. But they never have and likely never will. But despite that, most people, including me, thought Gov Cara had been okay.

She was tall, rail thin and her face was angular, with a sharp nose and chin. She had always kept her hair cut short and businesslike, which I always thought was the opposite of warm and welcoming. But whatever. It's her hair, right? Maybe it was for the no-nonsense, businesslike attitude she had always presented. Tonight, she wore a no-nonsense gray suit over a white silk blouse.

Coming in with her was Colonel Jefferson Wadsworth, the commandant of the Rhode Island State Police. He was wearing the uniform, minus the felt Stetson hat with the neat cleft in front. But his thigh-high boots were nicely polished. I wondered if he did the polishing, or left that to one of his orderlies.

Jonah stood up. Gus was already standing. I stayed seated because no one had said I could stand up.

"Gentlemen," the governor said, her voice with its usual harsh twang. She had grown up on the mean streets of Woonsocket, gone to Brown, married a wealthy money manager, dabbled herself in high finance and currency trading for a decade or so, and then decided to go into politics. At least she had plenty of funding.

"Please sit down."

Everybody who had a chair did.

"I have been discussing this case with Colonel Wadsworth," she said. "I told him I want it done right. No screw ups. We're talking about the sitting Attorney General of the state, and the overwhelming favorite to have been elected governor next month. So this investigation has to be done right."

She glanced over at Wadsworth, who nodded his agreement at her.

"To that end, I have instructed Colonel Wadsworth to appoint Mr. Julius Haddock as special adjunct to the Major Crimes bureau until this case is over," she said. "I want Chief Haddock on this case from the beginning. He did some excellent police work last summer when he solved a 30-year-old cold case from his town. I was very impressed with his abilities. I want him on this case."

Wadsworth cleared his throat.

"I am assigning Chief Haddock to partner with Jonah here," he said, his voice deep and measured. He probably practiced that in front of his bathroom mirror.

Jonah jumped to his feet. "You can't be serious!" he cried. "This guy is a possible suspect in this case. You can't assign him to be an investigator!"

"I can, and I have, Detective," the governor snapped. "I do not mean to imply that I don't have confidence in you or this department to conduct a successful homicide investigation. But the people of Rhode Island know that one of my best talents is finding and putting the right people in position to make positive change happen. I think Chief Haddock will be a great asset to your case and I want him on it."

Davis Ruggerio had listened to all this in silence, only his slightly arched eyebrows a giveaway to what he was thinking. Now, he cleared his throat.

"Governor," he said, "I agree that Chief Haddock did a good job with that old case. But this is something different. This is an open murder case, one day old. We don't have time to bring the chief up to date, read him into the case so far. That will cause a delay, and every homicide investigator knows that delays are deadly."

"Nonsense," Governor Romero said, smiling nicely at Ruggerio to dampen the harsh effect of her words. "It will take you two five minutes to bring the Chief up to date. In any case, this is not a subject up for debate. I want this to happen, and I expect you to make it happen. Do you understand?"

Davis looked at Jonah. Jonah looked at Davis. They both looked at Colonel Wadsworth, who stared back. The message was clear. It's done. Orders have been issued. Suck it up and get on with it.

Seeing that her point had been made, the governor walked out of the interview room, followed by Wadsworth. Jonah and Davis stared at the floor, frowning.

"This is bullshit," Jonah said, and stalked out of the room.

Davis looked at me. "We're interviewing the family members tomorrow morning," he said. "It's taking place at the officies of Edson Lane. Cynthia Knox insisted on her lawyer being there. I guess you should be there, too. Governor's orders."

"What time?" I said.

"Nine-thirty," he replied.

"I guess I'll see you then," I said.

Gus, standing behind me, slapped me on the back.

"Congratulations, Dad," he said. "I know you'll do a bang-up job."

CHAPTER 3

GUS DROVE ME home. When we walked in, Maggie Wells was sitting with Siggi. Maggie is Gus' intended and she was large with child, the baby due in January. The bottle of wine I had opened just before the storm troopers arrived was half gone. Since I knew Maggie wasn't likely to be drinking any, I figured Siggi had chugged down a few glasses.

She came up to me and wrapped me in her arms, as if holding on for dear life. I hugged her back. I understood how she must have felt, having lost me for nearly a year already, seeing me taken away again by law enforcement.

"It's OK," I said finally. "They just had some questions. I answered them. We're all good."

"Good?" Gus said with a chortle. "Hell, the Governor herself ordered Dad to join the task force working on the investigation!"

Siggi pulled her head back from my chest and looked at Gus. He nodded in confirmation.

"Maybe you should tell us what happened," Maggie said. She used to work for Preston Knox. She was one of his Knox's

Harem as the press liked to call the attorney general's office, staffed on purpose mostly by young women lawyers. She had also been named by Knox to the position of Special Master to oversee the Little Penwick Police Department during the aftermath of me being sent to jail and Gus being appointed the new chief. And she had also researched Knox's past history of sexual shenanigans with female co-workers, which was one reason why she got out of the law business and took up running an abused women's shelter program in Providence.

"Somebody got to Knox this morning," I told them. "Broke into his house and beat him to death with something. The staties wouldn't tell me what. Davis Ruggerio gave me the investigation notes but I haven't had time to read them yet."

"Was Cynthia there?" Maggie asked. I raised my eyebrows.

"His wife," she explained.

"Nobody said boo about the wife," I said. "But I'm supposed to be in attendance tomorrow morning when they interview the family. They got kids?"

"Two," Maggie said. "His daughter is probably off in college now. I don't know where. I wonder if they'd let her into Dartmouth after dear old dad got into trouble when he was there for slipping a roofie into a date's drink. He's got a son, too. I think he's in high school."

"Those poor kids," Siggi said. "Losing their father like that." She slurred the word 'those' a little, telling me where most of the wine had gone.

"Where was John Richardson?" Maggie asked next. "It was his job to keep Preston safe."

"He apparently had the morning off," I said. "He found the body when he showed up around ten."

"Huh," Maggie said.

"Huh, what?" I said. "You think Richardson might have done it?"

"No," Maggie said. "But Preston was tight with some unsavory characters. Maybe they called a special breakfast meeting for today, told Preston to tell John to come in late, and then …"

"Lot of speculation flying around the room," Gus said. "Absent any hard evidence. We should call it a night, all get a good night's rest and see where things stand in the morning. Davis Ruggerio is a pretty good cop. He'll make sure all the right questions get asked."

"What's this going to do to the election?" I asked. "I'm assuming Knox was favored to win, since he was a Democrat and we don't have any Republicans in this state. Does the lieutenant governor step up and run in his place?"

Maggie frowned. "I'd have to do some research into that," she said. "But I think that with the candidate for the office being rendered ineligible by virtue of death, the election for governor may get tossed over to the General Assembly, meeting in what they call a grand committee. They'll probably name Frannie O'Day, the candidate for lieutenant governor, to be the governor for the next term. But God only knows what the Rhode Island General Assembly will do."

Siggi was still holding on to me and didn't seem to want to let go. Gus and Maggie saw this and quickly said their good-nights and left. We stood there, listening to their footsteps, the sound of the car firing up and the tires crunching on the oyster shells as it backed up and drove away.

She swung around, buried her head in my neck and put her arms around my back.

"I'm a little drunk," she said into my neck. Her breath was warm and humid. "I couldn't stop drinking wine."

"Give me a few minutes and a couple of fingers of good Scotch, and I can get there with you," I said.

"Was it awful for you?"

"Not really," I said. "When I found out what they wanted, I knew it wasn't me. Then it was just a question of playing their little games. And I knew Gus was on the way. So I tried to find out what I could about who it was that offed Preston."

She pulled her head back and stared at me, eyes slightly unfocused.

"So you were playing your stupid cop games while I was here at home, worried sick?" she said, her tone slightly accusatory.

"I was trying to get some information," I said. "You can't build a case, either for the prosecution or the defense, until you understand the facts."

She thought about that, then buried her face in my neck again.

"Why don't we get you into bed," I said. "Things will look better in the morning."

I stooped down and slipped one arm behind her legs and scooped her up and carried her into the bedroom. I laid her down on the bed, pulled a light blanket over her. She had changed into comfortable after-work clothes when she came home from work and was barefoot. When I stood up, she was asleep, making those cute little moany sounds that women do instead of snoring.

I WENT BACK into the living room and turned on the TV. As expected, the coverage of the murder of Preston Knox, attorney general and probable governor-elect of Rhode Island, was wall to wall. I watched one of the Providence channels which had a ten-minute report, with a reporter standing outside Knox's home in Barrington, doing her stand-up. She had nothing new to report. But they had cut into the usual network programming, so you knew it was big news.

So I switched over to the cable news channels. The lefty ones—CNN and MSNBC—were talking about the murder and how it would affect the Democratic Party. They had the usual legions of talking heads coming on, talking about Preston Knox in tones of sad remembrance for this prince of the party, who had such a bright future ahead, whose name had been kicked around as an outside choice for President in two years and … I hit the mute button. None of them had any idea of what they were talking about. I checked with Fox News, but they just had their regular talking pundit on, and he was discussing the President with some other professional shit-talker. Apparently Fox didn't think the death of Preston Knox was going to affect the country greatly one way or another. I tended to agree with them on that.

I shut off the idiot box and sat there thinking for a while. My first thought—it had been my first thought from the moment they told me that Knox had been killed—was that the bent-nose boys up in Providence had decided to cut him loose. I knew they had not been happy when my son Gus, the chief of police, had busted up their little smuggling ring. Preston Knox's main job had been to prevent that from happening. He had failed.

On the other hand, I thought it would be foolish for the Family to cut loose a political figure on the verge of becoming governor. That would have been useful for the Family, to have the guv on their short leash. And the more I thought along those lines, the less I believed they had ordered a hit.

So who else could have done it? First rule of homicide: Look at the near-and-dear. But Knox's wife Cynthia had not even been home, apparently. That seemed to rule her out. Daughter away at college. The teen aged son was living at home, so he could be considered a possible suspect. But from what I understood, he had left to go off to school this morning and everything was fine and dandy with dear ole dad.

So if the family was ruled out, the list of possible suspects was long and kept getting longer the more I thought about it. John Robinson, who had a key the Knox home, was on the list. But nobody, including me, liked him for the murder. He was a cop, a cop with a cushy job, well paid and there wasn't a hint of conflict between the two men.

But then you had to start adding up all the people Knox had helped put behind bars in his six or seven years as AG.

That would be a long list. Then you could start adding in people he had defeated or pissed off—or both—in politics. Another long list, with probably some recent additions after his run for governor. You can't run for political office without ticking off somebody, especially here in Rhode Island. Then there were friends he cheated on the golf course, men whose wives he slept with, hell, maybe he had not paid his heating oil bill. There could be a lotta pissed off people out there.

I figured I could make more progress by making a list of everyone in Rhode Island wthout a good reason to knock off old Knox. There might be a couple of those.

By now, I was wishing I had been slugging back some Irish whiskey while I was thinking all this. But I hadn't. So I turned off the lights, locked the door, checked to make sure I hadn't left the oven on, and went to bed.

I WAS UP early the next morning —way before Siggi — and got busy. The law enforcement community in Rhode Island is pretty insular. We all know each other and, for the most part, are cooperative. For the most part: None of my brethren came publicly to my aid when I was railroaded into jail by the AG's office over a year ago; but everyone I talked to since had commiserated with me about the experience. I mostly understood. Nobody wanted to rock the boat in this uber-political state, and police politics is especially tricky these days, with idiots out there calling for defunding and other ways to crack down on the government jackboots..

I got Charlie Wexler on the phone a little after seven. He's been the chief of the Barrington PD for about fifteen years. It's a pretty good job: Barrington is a wealthy bedroom community just south of Providence. Lot of big homes, quiet neighborhoods, excellent schools thanks to the extensive tax base, and not much crime except for a little spillover from the nearby mean streets of Providence and East Providence.

"Jules!" Charlie said when I got him on the phone. "I don't think I've talked to you since you retired. How you likin' all the free time?"

"Free time? What's that?" I said with a chuckle. "I'm busier now than I was for the last twenty-four years."

"That's right," he said. "I heard you were doing some PI work. Bet that's interesting."

"Not always," I said. "Listen, what have you heard about the Knox case? They got any leads?"

"Not that they've shared with me," he said. "You know how the staties can be. They get their claws into a big case, they're gonna keep everyone else at arm's length. At least until they need help. Which they usually do, sooner or later."

"What happened?"

Charlie sighed. He was a big man. Moved slowly and ponderously. But he had a quick mind.

"Murder happened in front of the fireplace in his dining room," Charlie told me. "Killer picked up the poker from the fireplace tools and hit the poor guy in the head. Several times."

"Anger, huh?"

"Yeah, seems so," Charlie said.

"Prints?"

"From what I hear, they only picked up prints from family members. Wife, daughter, son and Knox himself, of course."

"And the wife wasn't home, right?"

He sighed again. "Apparently not," he said. "She was up in Boston for a few nights, staying with her mother. She's one of the Cabots up there, y'know."

"They're the ones speak only to God, right? In the land of the Bean and the Cod."

He chuckled. "That's what they say," he said.

"How about the kids?"

"Daughter Samantha is in her second year down at Penn," Charlie said. "She's been in Philly since August. Son Derek left the house at about 7:20 to catch the bus to Barrington High. He's an honor student and No. 2 on the golf team."

"And Daddy was fine when he left?"

"That's the word," Charlie said. "Although the family … Cynthia's family … has hired representation from Edson Lane for herself and the kids. Not sure why'd she do that. But then, her family is all lawyers and judges, so that's probably why."

"It's good to be the King," I said. "Or, failing that, to be filthy rich."

"So I've heard," Charlie said.

"Knowing what we know about some of Knox's associates, you think there's any connection to the goombahs in Providence?" I asked.

"That was my first thought," Charlie admitted. "You sleep with dogs, the fleas are gonna get you every time. But those guys wouldn't rub out someone all set to get elected governor in three and a half weeks. If they did have Knox in their dirty little claws, they wouldn't want to do anything to upset that, right? Plus, the publicity on this thing is going to be crazy, and the Family is still mostly allergic to operating in public. And if he had somehow managed to push their buttons … well, those people are not going to use a fireplace poker on the guy. Couple taps to the head and dropping him deep in some landfill is more their style."

"Yeah, there's that," I said. I had to agree with him. The Family guys had Preston Knox right where they wanted him: beholden, paid off and desperate to keep all that silent and out of public view. If he had ticked them off somehow, he would have been disappeared, not beaten to a bloody pulp in his own dining room.

"Speaking of publicity, you heard from the networks?"

"Oh, yeah," Charlie said with a sigh. "Supposed to do a stand-up for the Today Show in an hour. That'll be the first of many."

"Don't forget to smile," I said. "But thanks, Charlie, Appreciate the info."

"What's your interest, Jules?" he asked. Charlie Wexler's quick mind made itself evident again. "You gonna do a private drive-by on this one?"

"Actually," I said, "I've been appointed to the case. The Governor apparently liked my work on the Dixon cast last summer, and she told the staties to put me on the case."

"No shit?" Charlie said, exhaling. "I'll bet Colonel Wadsworth is bullshit about that."

"Him and every other trooper," I said. "I've got to keep one eye on my new partner, just in case he tries to nudge me into the path of a bus or something."

Wexler laughed. "Don't worry about that," he said, "The buses in Providence never run on time."

"Talk to ya later," I said and rang off.

Siggi came out of the bedroom, dark circles under her eyes and looking disheveled. I had already put the large bottle of Advil on the kitchen counter, next to the pot of coffee I had made earlier. She shook out two tablets and washed them down with some water, then poured herself a large mug.

"You let me drink too much last night," she said. "I feel awful."

I chuckled. "Wasn't me doing the pouring, babe," I said. "That would be your future daughter-in-law."

"I was worried," she said. "Maggie kept refilling my wineglass."

"Probably the best thing," I said. "She didn't want you to freak."

"I did anyway," she said. She sat down heavily at our table and drank some coffee. "Who were you talking to?"

"Charlie Wexler, chief up in Barrington," I said. "He gave me a few more details on the Knox case. But said the state boys are playing it close to the vest at the moment."

She nodded and drank more coffee. I got the distinct impression that, in her current condition, she had little to no craps to give about the Preston Knox murder.

"Listen," I said. "Do any of our immediate neighbors have a twelve or thirteen year-old boy?"

She studied her coffee mug for a moment or two, thinking.

"I don't think so," she said. "Why?"

"I was out on the deck yesterday afternoon, and this kid came by, stuck his head over the top of the fence," I told her. "Couldn't get him to say much. He asked if I was a cop. Then he got on his bike and rode away. Just wondered who it might have been."

She thought a moment longer, then shook her head.

"No idea," she said. "Nobody down the street has kids that age. But if he came on a bike, he could have come from anywhere."

She finished the last of her coffee and stood up with a groan.

"I'm going to take a long, hot shower," she said. "When I'm done, you may have to wait a while until the water heater makes more. Fair warning."

"Knock yourself out," I said. "I'll deal."

CHAPTER 4

A FEW HOURS later, I found myself sitting in a luxuriously upholstered chair that swiveled and rocked along the side of a magnificent mahogany table that ran nearly the entire length of the room. I was in the law offices of Edson Lane LLC, one of the whitest of the white-stocking law firms in the city, in a conference room looking down on the city from the heights of the fourteenth floor (which is pretty high for Providence).

Three of us were sitting in a group at one end of the table: Davis Ruggerio, Jonah Allen and me. Edson Lane had given us all a cup of coffee, which was dark roast and excellent, and put out some cookies. Davis and Jonah had opted out—probably didn't want to get sugar on their fingers—but I had put a couple on my plate. Us old cops know that when someone gives you free food, you should take it.

After making us wait for a few minutes, the passive-aggressive way to show us who was in charge, the elegantly dressed figure of Charles Elkington, Esquire walked into the room. One of the partners in the firm, he wore a thousand-dollar suit, perfectly fitted to every nook and cranny of his still quite fit body. His tie knot was immaculate, his cufflinks sparkled in the office light, every strand of his salt-and-pepper hair was pomaded into place and his toothy smile was bright and well polished.

"Gentlemen," Elkington said, standing at the far end of the table from where we sat, "I'd like to establish some ground rules for this meeting."

"How about you bring in the members of the Knox family and let us ask them questions," Jonah Allen said, trying —and failing — to keep the exasperation out of his voice. "This is a murder investigation, not some tort about tripping over the carpet in a retail store."

Elkington didn't blink. I started watching his eyelids because I wanted to see if he *ever* blinked.

"Thank you, Detective Allen," he said. "I will bring in each member of the Knox family in due course. Mrs. Knox has asked me to sit in on your interview session in order to protect her children."

"From what?" Davis Ruggerio snapped.

"To protect their civil rights," Elkington replied. "And to make sure they do not make any incriminating comments."

"So which one killed Preston?" I said.

Elkington looked at me with perfectly arched eyebrows. "I beg your pardon?" he said.

"You said you want to make sure they don't incriminate themselves," I said. "That sounds like one of them is the guilty party in this case. So … which one is it? Save us all a lot of time. Of course, only one of us is billing their time out at, what? Six hundred an hour?"

The lawyer's face colored slightly. No lawyer likes to be reminded that his time is billable. Makes them seem like rapacious money grubbers. Which, of course, many of them are.

"I think you will find that none of my clients has the slightest culpability in this matter," he said. "I do not think it unusual for a witness to be allowed to have representation on hand during an interview with law enforcement."

"Whatever, Charlie," Ruggerio said, waving his hand. "Bring them in, please. We'll talk with the mother, first. Then the two kids."

Elkington nodded gravely and went to the door. He stuck his head outside and made a motion. In a few moments, he stepped back, held the door open and allowed Cynthia Knox to enter.

She was wearing a pinkish knit suit with two-inch heels and a lacy cravat thing at her neck, the ends of which hung down. Her golden brown hair was coiffed into a non-moving mass on her head and she smiled at us as she entered.

"Good morning," she said, "I'm Cynthia Knox." She walked down to our end of the table and gravely shook hands with all of us. Then she went back to the other end and sat down next to Charlie Elkington.

Davis put his pocket tape recorder on the table and clicked it on.

He stated the date, the time, his name and those of Jonah and me. "This interview is being conducted with Ms. Cynthia Knox, wife of the deceased victim, and Mr. Charles Elkington, her attorney of record from the firm of Edson Lane." He paused, looked at Jonah and me, and nodded, "Go ahead Jonah," he said.

"Miz Knox," Jonah said, "You were not at home on the morning your husband was killed, is that correct?"

"Yes."

"Can you tell us please where you were?"

"I had been in Boston for two days prior to … prior to that day," she said. "My mother, who is in her eighties, is not well and I had gone to stay with her to provide what assistance I could."

"Did you frequently go to Boston to stay with family?" Allen asked.

"I don't know about 'frequently,'" she said, "But yes, I have spent several nights in the last six months with my mother."

"What's wrong with her?" I asked.

She looked at me. "What do you mean?"

"You say you have spent several nights with her in Boston because she is not well. What is wrong with her?"

Cynthia fixed me with her dark eyes ablaze. "She is eighty-six," she said. "Her mobility is not great. She needs a walker to move from room to room. She needs assistance with most of her daily activities."

"Don't the servants handle all of that?"

Her glare deepened, along with the color of her cheeks. "I'm not sure what you mean," she said.

I sighed. She was playing hardball.

"Okay," I said. "Does your mother employ a chef?"

"Yes."

"Does she employ a maid?"

"Yes."

"Is the maid a sleep-in, or does she come and go every day?"

"Juanita has her own room," Cynthia said.

"Does your mother employ a driver?"

"Yes."

"Gardener? Private nurse? Private secretary?"

"I'm not sure what you're driving at, Chief Haddock," Elkington tried to sound outraged. "Mrs. Cabot is a wealthy woman, but I'm not sure what that has to do with the matter at hand."

"I'm driving at the witness's statement that she went to Boston on this and several other occasions in the past year to, and I quote, 'to provide what assistance I can' to her mother." I said. "It sounds to me like her mother employs a large staff of people paid to provide her with all the assistance she needs. So I'd like to know the real reason Mrs. Knox left her home on several occasions, including the few days before her husband's murder. Because I don't think the excuse she's given will hold water."

Cynthia Knox looked at Elkington, who sat up a little straighter, back arched.

"Surely, Chief Haddock," he said in his best lecturing tone, "The important question is who killed Preston Knox. My client's testimony is that she was not at home when that crime occurred. She is testifying that she was in Boston at the time. That fact can easily be verified by asking Mrs. Knox's mother or any of her household staff. The reasons why she was in Boston strikes me as completely irrelevant."

"We will ask the questions, counselor," Jonah Allen said. "Please instruct your client to answer them truthfully. The relevance or lack thereof will be determined by us."

"Very well," Elkington said. "Continue."

"When was the last time you spoke to your husband?" Davis Ruggerio asked.

She looked at him for a moment, thinking.

"I — I really can't remember," she said. "Probably the night before he …" She stopped. "We generally spoke in the evenings when I was not at home. I probably called him that night, asked about the campaign, asked how Davy was."

"Would you say that your marriage to Preston Knox was a happy one?" Jonah asked.

Elkington jumped all over that one.

"I must object!" he said loudly. "Again, what relevance can their be to the matter at hand, which is the murder of Preston Knox?"

"Because, counselor," Allen said, "If the Knox marriage was an unhappy one—if, for example, if one of the spouses was constantly running home to mother—that might indicate some kind of antagonism between the parties. And we are trying to determine who might have a motive to commit murder. Or arrange to have their spouse eliminated."

"That is an outrageous accusation," Elkington was still flogging his outrage horse, urging it on with sharpened spurs. "I must object in the strongest possible terms."

"Answer the question," David Ruggerio said sternly. The chief of detectives for the Major Crimes bureau carried an unmistakable aura of authority.

"We were happily married," Cynthia Knox said. "We had our fair share of disagreements. Every marriage does. But Preston and I were committed, long term, to each other."

"So there were no plans for you two to begin to dissolve your marriage after the election?" I said.

She turned on me like a cornered feral cat.

"Who told you that?" she snapped. "Who? It's not true!"

Davis decided to lower the temperature in the room, which was getting up to the smoking hot level.

"Mrs. Knox, can you describe the relationship your late husband had with his two children?," he said. "Did they get along?"

Cynthia was still glaring at me with red spots of anger on her cheeks. Slowly, she made herself stop glaring, and turned to look at Davis.

"We were … *are* … a happy family," she said. "Samantha, my daughter, was the apple of her daddy's eyes. She is studying pre-law at Pennsylvania, and intends to follow in her father's footsteps in the law. They have always been very close."

She paused and slipped a white tissue out of her sleeve and used it to briefly wipe her nose.

"David and his father were not quite as close, but Preston was always very proud of his son. He does well at school, plays on the golf team and has lots of good friends. We're not sure, yet, what career path lies ahead for Davie, but he's just a sophomore in high school. There's still plenty of time for him to find his way."

"Do either one of your children have anger issues?" Jonah asked.'

"Whatever do you mean?" Cynthia sounded nonplussed.

"Do they have anger management problems?" Jonah persisted. "Bursts of uncontrolled anger? Hitting out? Throwing things?"

"Good heavens, no," Cynthia said, smiling a little. "That sounds perfectly dreadful. No, they are both very normal teenagers."

"Does Samantha have a boyfriend?" I asked. "Is she dating anyone down there at Penn?"

Cynthia dabbed at her nose again with the tissue. I was ten feet away, across the well-polished mahogany table, but I thought I could see her eyes widen just a bit.

"No," she said after a brief pause. "She has not told me if she is seriously dating anyone. She is just nineteen, almost twenty. She knows she needs good grades to get into a prestigious law firm. I don't think she'd risk all that over some boy."

"Would she tell you if she was?" I pressed.

She looked at me again, not in a friendly way.

"Of course," she said. "I'm her mother."

"You said David had lots of friends at school," I said. "Do any of them come over to your home a lot?"

"Sometimes," she nodded. "The last two years, when he's been at Barrington High, his circle of friends is mainly the boys on the golf team. Several of those boys live in our neighborhood and their families are members of the country club, as are we. So if they are not practicing or playing, they hang out with each other at the club, or at some of our homes. He has had his friends over from time to time to watch golf tournaments and play video games."

"Can you give us some of their names?" Allen pressed.

Cynthia looked offended, but she gave Jonah four or five names of boys. He wrote them down in his notebook.

"Would any of those boys have reason to be angry with Preston about anything?" I asked. "Anything he might have said or done?"

Cynthia thought for a moment or two, then shook her head.

"Not that I can think of," she said. "Preston was not home very much. He was very busy with his work as attorney general. He may have been at home when Davie's friends came over, but I can't really recall a specific instance."

"Did Preston go watch your son play golf for Barrington?" I asked. "Did he go to the games?"

"Tournaments," Cynthia sniffed, correcting me. "The interscholastic golf tournaments are usually held on weekday afternoons after school. Like from three or three-thirty. Preston never had much opportunity to attend those, although he did go to the state tournament last spring, which was on a Friday, I think."

"So, no, he didn't go to see your son play," I said.

She glared at me, but didn't answer.

"Again, gentlemen," Elkington piped in, probably to convince Cynthia that he was earning his billable hours. "I fail to see the relevance ..."

"And again, counselor," Allen cut him off. "We will ask the questions, relevant or not. This is an investigation, not a trial."

"Mrs. Knox," Davis Ruggerio said. "Can you tell us of anyone you think might have had the motive to kill your husband? Friends, family, colleagues. business associates? Anyone you can think of who might have done this?"

She looked at Davis with relief and gratitude in her eyes.

"No," she said. "I have been thinking about nothing else since I heard the news. Who could have done such a thing to my Preston? I'm sorry, but I have been unable to think of anyone."

She looked at us and teared up a little. Her white tissue was put to use again.

"Thank you, Mrs. Knox," Davis said. "I apologize if some of our questions seemed abrupt. We are trying to eliminate all possibilities as we investigate this case."

She nodded her thanks at him.

"Mr. Elkington," Davis said, "We'd like to interview the children next."

"Can I stay for that?" Cynthia said, looking at Elkington. "I am their mother and ..."

"I'm sorry, Mrs. Knox," Ruggerio said. "But we are going to insist that you not be present. Having their mother in the room may cause Samantha and David to withhold some important information. We are not trying to pull a fast one on anyone. We're just trying to get to the truth."

Despite Cynthia's entreating looks, Elkington nodded.

"Very well," he said. "Cynthia, I will be here the entire time. I will not let them browbeat those kids, I promise you."

Cynthia, finally, nodded and stood up. Elkington leaped to his feet to open the conference room door for her and followed her out. In half a minute or so, he came back, this time trailed by the two Knox kids.

CHAPTER 5

"G_ENTLEMEN_," E_LKINGTON_ _ANNOUNCED_ rather grandly when he came back into the room. "Allow me to introduce you to Samantha Knox and her brother David."

The three of us stood up as Samantha came down to our side of the table. I shook her hand. It was damp, no doubt due to anxiety. She was a tall girl, right around six feet, and her body was still in the process of shedding her high school baby fat. She had straight hair, down to her shoulders, of a golden brown shade, just like her mother's. She gave me a nervous smile, looking as if she wondered what the hell this was all about. She was wearing a print dress, knee length, and sensible black shoes. She looked every inch the Ivy League co-ed.

Her younger brother David plopped himself down at an empty chair next to Elkington. He had his phone out and was staring at it, occasionally reaching a finger up to swipe the screen. He didn't look at us or acknowledge our presence in any way. He was wearing jeans with strategic rips and tears here and there in the fabric, and a fleece sweatshirt. Dirty sneakers. His hair was longish and uncombed, also a golden brown shade. He had Preston Knox's face, the same distinguished nose, arching eyebrows and square jaw. With a little adolescent acne spotted here and there.

"David," said Davis Ruggerio, "Do you mind putting your phone away for this interview? We'd like to have your full attention, please."

David said nothing, did not remove his eyes from his screen. He continued to swipe on it, apparently in the middle of a game of some kind. His sister went over and sat down next to him and put her hand on his arm gently.

"D?" she said.

He sighed and put the phone screen down on the table. He crossed his arms across his chest and stared at us defiantly.

"Thank you," Davis said. He repeated his preamble for the tape recorder, listing the names of everyone in the room, the time and date, and began.

"Miz Knox," he began. He looked at her with a smile. "May I call you Samantha?"

She smiled back and nodded.

"You are in your second year at Penn, is that right?"

"Yes," she said.

"Pre-law?"

She nodded.

"Doing OK so far? Grades OK?"

"Not bad," she said. "My GPA is three point seven something. I had a math class last year and only got a B-plus. Other than that, things are OK."

"That's great," Davis said, trying to put the girl at ease. "I never got much over three when I was in school."

David made a little scoffing noise.

"Have you made some friends at school?" Davis continued.

"Oh, sure," Samantha said. "There's a tight group of us in the pre-law sequence. We all live in the same dorm and pretty much hang together."

"Any boyfriends?"

Her face reddened a little.

"Ah … well … let's just say no one real serious right now," she said. "I've been trying to keep the old nose to the grindstone. Daddy told me that I had to keep my grades near the top of the class, so I could get admitted to one of the best law schools."

"So you're planning to go into law," Davis said. "Just like your Dad."

She nodded. "It's been our dream all along," she said.

"Barf," her brother said, sitting next to her.

"Shut up, D" she hissed at him.

"You were not at home when your father … when the incident with your father occurred," Jonah Allen took over.

"No," she said. "I was at school."

"When was the last time you were home?"

"I left Rhode Island at the end of August," she said. "Classes began September first. I haven't been back home since. I was planning to come back for the election, of course."

"Did you work on the campaign?" I asked.

She looked at me. "Of course," she said. "All summer long. It was very busy. There's so much that needs to be done on a campaign. You have no idea."

"What's the name of your dorm?" Jonah cut in.

She looked at him. "Gregory House," she said.

"Roommate?"

"I live in a quad room," she said. "So I have three other roommates." She reeled off the names. Allen wrote them down.

"Can you think of anyone who might have wanted to harm your father?" Allen asked.

She shook her head.

"No one from the campaign said anything that might have sounded threatening?"

Another shake of the head.

"No," she said, "I really can't. I mean, I know he was the attorney general, and that means some people didn't like him, or were opposed to him and stuff like that. But I can't think of anyone I know who would have done something like that."

I nodded. "And your relationship with your father was OK?" I said.

"Oh, yes," she said quickly. "Daddy and I were very close. He helped me get into Penn. He was going to come down for a football game after the election ..." Her voice broke at the end and her eyes teared up. Elkington pushed a box of tissues over in front of her and she took one out.

I turned to David. "What about you, young man?" I asked. "Any thoughts on enemies your Dad might have had?"

"About half the state," he said, eyes narrowed. "Republicans, the Mob, everyone he put in jail, my uncle Rob ..." He was counting off his fingers as he made his list.

"David," his sister gasped. "Don't say that!"

I held up my hand in a stop signal.

"OK," I said, "Let's go over that list. I get it that Republicans didn't like your Dad. He was a Democrat and he was about to be elected governor. But do you know of any Republicans specifically who wanted to kill your dad?"

He glowered at me, but eventually shook his head.

"Right," I said. "I think we can put the Mob and everyone he put in jail in the same boat. Possible suspects, but unlikely, for a variety of reasons. But tell me more about this Uncle Rob."

"He's Mom's older brother," Samantha said. "Lives up in Boston. He and my Dad never really got along. Dad once told me that Rob didn't approve of my Mom marrying him, and there's been friction between them ever since."

"What does Uncle Rob do for a living?" I asked.

"He's a judge," David said, smirking at me. "Federal. Lifetime appointment. Probably crooked as all the rest up there."

Samantha rolled her eyes.

"Has Uncle Rob been in contact with your Dad anytime recently?" I asked.

"I dunno," David said. "They never tell us anything."

"Who doesn't? Your parents?"

He smirked at me again. "Duh."

"You were one of the last people to see your Dad alive,"I said. "Want to tell me what went down that morning before you left for school?"

David shrugged, that infuriating teenage signal of dismissal and feigned disinterest.

"Same as every other day," he said. "I got up, went down to the kitchen to have some breakfast. Dad was already up, drinking coffee and talking on the phone."

"You remember with whom?"

He smirked again. "With whom? How the hell would I know? I assumed it was somebody from the campaign. That's the only people he talked to. The campaign."

"You don't sound like you liked the idea of your Dad running for governor," I said.

He shrugged again. Smirking and shrugging were his go-to expressions.

"Politics is bullshit," he said. "Politicians say they'll do all this stuff, and then they don't. He was just like all the others."

Samantha was watching her brother with the watchful, narrowed eyes of a hawk on the hunt. Her face had reddened somewhat and she looked like she wanted to reach over and box his ears or something.

"Who is your best friend?" I asked. David looked at me, like he couldn't believe I'd ask something like that.

"Say again?" he said.

"Your best friend," I said. "Your mother said you have several buds from high school. Which one do you hang with the most?"

He was silent, thinking about that.

"I dunno," he said. "I hang with lots of guys. Don't know if there's one I'd say is my best friend."

"Oh, for Pete's sake, D," his sister said, "You know it's Danny Kuhn. You guys have been inseparable since fifth grade."

"So, Danny Kuhn is your best friend," I said.

David nodded. "Okay," he said. "I guess."

"You talk with him about stuff?"

"I guess," he said. "Sometimes."

"Talk about girls?"

He was suspicious. "What about them?"

"I mean, you talk about some of the girls in school. Who's cute. Who's interesting. Who's smokin' hot. Stuff like that."

"Yeah, sure," he said, eyes narrowed. He didn't know where I was going with this, and didn't like it.

"So if your Dad was spending a lot of time on the campaign, Danny Kuhn is maybe one of your friends you would talk to about that, about how it made you feel."

David scoffed. "We really don't sit around talking about our feelings," he said. "He's on the golf team with me, so we mostly talk about practice, the match coming up, our golf swings … stuff like that."

"And girls," I said.

He gave me a short smile and a nod.

"OK," I said, "Let's go back to that morning. You come downstairs, get some breakfast and your Dad is sitting there, talking to his campaign. Did he say anything to you?"

David started to shrug, but stopped mid-shrug. "I think he said good morning and that I'd better hurry up or I'd be late for the bus."

"Was that true?" I asked. "Were you running late that morning?"

"Not any more than any other morning," he said. "I had plenty of time to get to the bus stop. He was just hassling me. He did that practically every day of my life."

"OK," I said. "What happened next?"

He shrugged again. "I grabbed some toast, checked my phone for any email, DMs, whatever. Then I went upstairs, got dressed, got my backpack, came downstairs, said bye and left."

"Was he still talking on the phone to his campaign?"

"I think he hung up at some point," the kid said. "Don't really remember."

"Did you make it?" I asked.

"Make what?"

"The bus. Were you late?"

He smiled. "Naw. Bus was late again. Had plenty of time. As usual."

"Did you see anyone outside the house?" I asked. "Any strange cars parked on the street or in the driveway?"

He started to shake his head no, but then stopped.

"What?" I said.

"I was going to say no, but I just remembered there was a cable truck in front of Mr. Hayes' house," he said. "I think it was a cable truck. It was a white van, ladders on the top. I just assumed they were from the Cox Cable people. It was just before seven thirty, I think. I don't know if those guys get started that early in the morning."

"That's good," I said encouragingly. "Was there someone in the truck? In the back, maybe?"

He shook his head.

"Naw," he said. "I don't remember seeing anyone. Just the truck."

"What is Mr. Hayes' name?" I asked.

"Jonathan," Samantha said. "Mr. and Mrs. Jonathan Hayes. Her name is Stephanie and they have two kids around seven and five. Betsy and Adam." She smiled at me. "I baby sat for them all through high school."

"Good," I said. "Thank you. See? We've spent just ten minutes with you two and we have a couple good leads to follow up on."

Samantha smiled at me, relieved and seemed happy to have been of some help. David stared at me without expression, his crossed leg swinging wildly back and forth under the table.

THE THREE OF us rode back to state police headquarters on the Danielson Pike west of downtown Providence in Davis Ruggerio's sedan. It had a comfortable back seat, as opposed to a regular squad car which had a back seat encased in unbreakable plexiglass.

"I'm gonna call Billy Donovan," Davis Ruggerio said as he drove us along the city streets. Both Jonah Allen and I knew that Donovan was the ASAC, the Assistant Special Agent in Charge of the Providence field office of the FBI. He reported to the head guy up in Boston.

"We need someone to check out the girl's story in Philly," he said. "Talk to her RA, some of her friends, her teachers. The feds can handle that a lot quicker than we can. And Billy has already volunteered any help we need from him."

Jonah and I nodded.

"What about that cable TV truck?" I asked. "That check against what the neighbors said?" The state police had already spoken to all the neighbors on Preston Knox's street. Their interviews were in the case report I had seen.

"We'll send someone back over to talk to the Hayes family," Davis said. "See if we can pin that down."

"I know a guy at the cable company," I said. "He can look at their schedule sheet, tell us if one of their trucks was on that street that morning."

"We'll look into it," Davis said, and cast a glance back at me in his rearview. *Don't press it*, his look said.

"I can go up to Boston and talk to Uncle Rob," I said. "Jonah can go find this Kuhn kid and see if Junior's story matches up."

Jonah turned to look at me in the back seat.

"You think the kid is lying?" he said.

"Don't know," I said. "I got the feeling all three of them were blowing a good quantity of smoke in there. Did you guys pick up on that?"

Davis nodded. "There is certainly a weird family dynamic going on," he said. "I didn't get a whole lot of sadness from any of them that dear old dad is gone."

"Exactly," I said. "Especially the wife. I wonder what is going on with her? Do we have the telephone records from Knox's phone? I'd like to know when Cynthia called him. And I'd like to know who Preston was talking with that morning, before he was killed."

"We subpoena-ed Knox's phone call list," Davis said. "We can do the same for Cynthia and the kids, maybe. But there might be pushback, which would be a shitstorm. I'll talk with Colonel Wadsworth, see if he agrees."

"Fine," I said. "I know there are political considerations to worry about. We had them down in Little Penwick, too."

Jonah made a scoffing sound.

We rode in silence for a few minutes.

"What else?" Davis said when we were almost at the HQ building.

"I'm lining up interviews with the campaign staff," Jonah said. "The DNC guy from Washington is due in town tomorrow or the next day, and I'm planning to sit down with him, see what I can learn about the dynamics of the campaign. Many of the professional staffers have already switched over to Senator Blackford's campaign, but I'll get to them as well."

"If you need any help with that, let me know," I said. He looked back at me again, with a smirk on his face. *When hell freezes over*, he seemed to be saying.

I let it go. He was still mad about me being appointed to the investigation. His investigation. We'd probably have to have it out one day, but I decided later was better than now.

CHAPTER
6

BACK AT HEADQUARTERS, I found an empty desk in the large squad room. I sifted through the notebook binder containing the official case record so far—the so-called 'murder book'—then went back and found the name of the campaign manager for Knox's campaign. Her name was Betsey Levine, who I vaguely knew was one of the Rhode Island's top political movers. When not running campaigns, she was often seen and heard being a lobbyist for some organization or other, and always turned up in the news when the state legislature was debating some important issue. I found a note saying she had already switched over to work for the Blackman campaign.

I called the campaign office of Senator Harold Blackman, running for his fourth, or was it fifth? term as our state's senior senator. He was running against a thirty-year-old Libertarian who wanted to make all narcotics legal and end the income tax, to be replaced by a national sales tax. Blackman was favored to win re-election by sixty points. At least.

"It's a beautiful Blackman day," the receptionist said when she answered my call. "How can we make your life better today?"

"Is Betsey Levine working there today?" I said.

"Hold please," she said and I listened to bad Muzak for about ten minutes. Finally, there was a click.

"This is Betsey," said a female voice.

I introduced myself, said I was with the state police investigation into Preston Knox's murder and asked if she had time to answer a few questions.

"Julius Haddock. Aren't you the chief of police in Little Penwick?" she asked.

"Used to be," I said. "Retired now. But Governor Romero appointed me to the state police task force investigation."

"Well, good for you," she said. "How can I help?"

"When was the last time you spoke to Preston Knox?"

"I guess it was the morning he was murdered," she said. "We spoke almost every morning at around six. We're both early risers and it was a good time to discuss the campaign without being interrupted."

"How long did you speak?"

"I'd say about a half hour," she said. "That was our usual habit. I'd go over the day's planned events, give him any background he needed on the people he was going to meet with that day, just get him prepped and ready."

"I see," I said. "So there was nothing unusual about your conversation that day?"

"Not that I can recall," she said. "Just our usual morning call."

"Was there anything you discussed that morning that seemed upsetting to Knox? Anything he was upset about?"

"No," she said. "The campaign was running well. All signs were good."

"You weren't talking to him around seven, seven-fifteen?"

"I don't think so," she said. "It was more like between six and six-thirty. That's not an exact time of the call, but it's around the time I remember."

I paused. I had another question to ask, but wasn't sure how to ask it. The hell with it, I thought, let 'er fly!

"Was Preston having an affair with any of his staff workers?" I said.

There was a long silence on the other end.

"Wow," she said. "That was direct."

"Sorry," I said, "Couldn't think of any way to sugarcoat it."

"Well," she said, "I don't usually follow my staff around to see who they're screwing, as a matter of course. And I do deliver 'The Talk' at the beginning of every campaign, in which I warn people that having flings with each other, while fun and all, can be harmful to the campaign in the long run. I encourage them, rather strongly, not to do it."

"You tell Preston that too?" I asked.

She laughed. "I expect he knew what to do and what not to do," she said. "Not his first rodeo."

"You haven't answered my question," I said. "Was he screwing anybody? He had a certain reputation as a Lothario."

"Lothario?" she laughed again. "What a quaint term."

"I am nothing if not quaint," I said. "So, was he?"

Betsey Levine sighed. She wanted to lie. I could almost feel it. But she also realized that I was an official representative of law enforcement, and she knew lying to the cops was always a bad idea that could come back to bite you. And if she lied to me about this, and then it turned out to be true, it would reflect badly on her. And as a political op, she wanted to stay on as many good sides as she could.

"I think there were two," she said finally. On my side of the call, I pumped my fist. Yes!

"Names?"

She sighed again. "Do you really have to do this?" she said. "They're just kids. Might be tough on them, knowing their love lives are all public knowledge."

"We're investigating a murder," I said. "Of a guy who was going to be our next governor. We'll be as gentle as we can, but there might have been a jealous boyfriend or father or brother who took exception to Preston fooling around with their little flower."

She thought about that for a bit. "Yeah, I get it," she said finally. "The two girls I suspected Preston was canoodling with were Camilla DeRosa and Angie Sagassian. Both were campaign volunteers, poli-sci majors at Providence College. Weird thing is I think they know each other, but I don't know if they knew their friend was also sleeping with the candidate. I try to stay way out of my staff's sex lives. It can get icky."

"Do you think Preston Knox and his wife had a happy marriage?" I asked.

She sighed again.

"No idea," she said. "Guessing not. The two little campaign hotties is just one indication. But I watched the two of them together at campaign functions. There was a coolness there. Like 'let's do this and get it over with.'"

"When did you first meet Preston Knox?"

"I think it was before his campaign for AG," she said. "I had met him briefly at various campaign and party events, but he asked me to lunch and told me he wanted to run and asked if I would manage his campaign. He told me I was the best at what I did."

She laughed a bit.

"Of course, he was right. I am the best. I got him elected and re-elected four years later."

"I imagine he, err, made a move on you, too?"

She laughed again. It was a pleasant sound, that laugh.

"Oh, hell yes," she said. "But it was almost funny. Like he felt he had to make a pass at me, to keep his male membership card or something, His heart really wasn't in it. I told him not to be a damn fool, I wasn't going to sleep with him, like ever. And for a million years after that. Once that was out of the way, we got along pretty well over the years."

She paused. "I've seen his type all my life," she said. "Big, important guys. They read their own press clippings and get to believing them. Think they're immortal. Think the world, or their little parts of it, can't possibly exist without them in charge. And they think that every woman they meet is overcome by their unquenchable sexual attraction and wants to suck their wee-wee. Well, I didn't, and I told him so. After that, it was cool."

"Tell me about the girls," I said.

There was another pause. "Camilla was assigned to the GOV squad," she said. "Get Out the Vote," she explained. "Working with the various communities around the state to help people vote. Voter reg drives, coordinate rides to the polls, organizing the phone banks, some work on absentee ballots ... that kind of stuff."

I nodded. "And Angie?"

"PR and communications," she said. "She was ...is ... a looker. So we made sure she was out there front and center. She was working as press liaison, so if Joe Reporter from Woonsocket or someplace had a question about a policy position or something, he'd call Angie and she's send him the material he needed." She paused. "Of course, the main political reporters—from the Projo, the TV stations and the national press—they all called me for statements and information. Part of my job."

She stopped, thinking about something, and then laughed, mostly to herself. "It's funny," she said. "There are always two or three male reporters, the local ones, who get smitten with someone on the campaign like Angie. You notice: They ask about Preston's position on the car tax. Then a couple days later, it's about his position on climate change. This goes on for a few days, and you eventually realize that he's not writing any stories. He's just coming up with excuses to talk to Angie." She laughed, shaking her head. "Sometimes they get brave and ask for a date, but mostly they just come to press conferences and stare at Angie." I heard her sigh. "You men are so predictable."

"Probably so," I said. "Unlike you women, who are ciphers."

"'Ciphers?'" she said with a chuckle. "I think I've been called worse names. But I'm not sure."

"Are Camilla and Angie still around?" I asked. "Did they move over here to Blackford's campaign with you? Or did they go back to school?"

"No, they've flown the coop, went back to school," Betsey said. "Back to the ordinary and humdrum life of everyone else. What was it Emerson said, 'Lives of quiet desperation?'"

"That's me all over," I said, "Quietly desperate. Thanks for your time, Ms. Levine. Can I call you again if something else comes up?"

"I think I'd like that," she said. "Just ask for the cipher."

I called Davis Ruggerio.

"Got some names that might be interesting," I said. "Just talked to Betsey Levine, Knox's campaign manager, and she told me he might have been humping a couple young staffers."

"Geez," Davis said. "The guy really was a sleazeball, wasn't he?"

"The best," I said. "Or the worst, might be more accurate."

"Gimme the names," Davis said. I did.

"We'll check it out," he said.

IT WAS WEDNESDAY, which meant it was a Jack's Diner day.

At lunchtime, I drove back down down to Little Penwick and made my way to Burr's Village and Jack's decrepit little lunch spot up on the hill overlooking the mill pond and the old grist mill. For about a year now, I had made it a habit to meet three of my old friends here on Wednesday for lunch and gossip. Junior Hastings, the current proprietor and absolutely no relation to the original Jack, put up with us and probably enjoyed having at least four regular customers in the middle of the week. He would prepare sandwiches for us, often with a cup of soup, and toss in some kind of dessert at the end. If we felt like it, we'd grab a cold Bud out of Junior's cooler behind the bar. Afterwards, there was coffee, of course. And the four of us would each throw a twenty on the counter when we left. Probably way too much for what we got, but then, we didn't have to spend a lot of time thinking about what to order and could use that time on the talk and gossip part. It worked.

The other three guys were already there when I arrived and I grabbed my beer and joined them at the round table near the window. Some of the maples and poplars around the mill pond had begun to turn colors and it looked all nice and New Englandy out there, despite the cloud cover.

"Howdy, chief," said Billy Church when I walked in. Billy ran the eponymous insurance agency on the edge of the village green, the third generation of Church's to do so. And his daughter was in the process of taking over the business and becoming the fourth.   "Have you ever seen a shit show like this? The Providence *Journal* had a headline about the same size as the one they used when Kennedy got shot. Every story in the front section was something about Preston Knox. Incredible!"

"All the news that fits," I said, sitting down and nodding to the other guys.

"I gotta tell ya, Julius," said Harlan Bailey, "When I heard a couple nights ago that Knox had been killed, I told the wife that I hoped it wasn't you. I mean, we all knew how you felt about that guy." Harlan ran a large auto repair shop down on the East Highway, sold a few junkers on the side and had long ago tied up the town's school bus, snowplow and Public Works truck repair concessions. He was doing pretty well these days, and probably had not had his hands inside an engine for more than ten years. He could now afford to hire the best mechanics instead, so he did.

I nodded. "The state police hauled me over to Portsmouth, gave me the third degree," I said. "Gus showed up and swore I had not been in Barrington yesterday morning, so they had to let me go."

"I woulda crapped my pants," said Ben Almy, the last of us four amigos. Ben was retired now, after putting in his thirty-five years as an engineer at the big defense plant over in Middletown where they made radar and torpedo systems for the newest submarines in the Navy's fleet. He had also been my first customer when I turned private eye after retiring and going to jail. Unfortunately, he had suspected that his wife was fooling around on him, and that case did not end particularly well when it turned out she wasn't. Still, we had buried the hatchet and all seemed back to normal again.

"But the good news is that after they tried pulling out my fingernails one at a time, the governor walked in and ordered the Staties to add me to their investigation team," I said. "So I went from 'probably guilty' to 'Yessir, Mr. Haddock, sir.' There's one guy on the team that still hasn't recovered yet."

"Damn," Billy Church said, exhaling the word. "That's the strangest thing I ever heard! You have some secret photos of Gov. Romero, or what?"

"Ewww," said Harlan. "Now I can never unsee that!"

We all laughed.

"I mean, killing the attorney general and the presumptive governor..." Ben shook his head. "Do they know who did it yet?"

I shook my head. "Not yet," I said. I told them that I had spoken with Charlie Wexler, the chief up in Barrington, and related what he had told me.

"Who do you think it was, Jules?" Billy Church asked.

"No idea," I said. "A public figure like that, guy like Preston Knox, the list is pretty long. We talked with members of the Knox family this morning—the widow and their two kids. There's a few things to follow up on. Time will tell."

"I just hope the news stops talking about it before the weekend," Harlan said. "Pats got the Jets this weekend. Who you putting your shekels on?"

"I think if I ever wagered on a team from New York, I'd have to give up my membership as a New Englander," I said.

"Could not agree more," Harlan said. "But you'd be nuts to bet anything on the Pats. I think Coach Bill has finally gone over to the Dark Side."

"When was he *not* on the Dark Side?" asked Ben Almy. "Belichick has always been a strange bird."

We all nodded in agreement. The Patriots' head coach was not lacking in weirdness, but he was also not lacking in Super Bowl rings, so we tended to forgive him his weirdness.

Junior brought out the soup and sandwiches and we dug in with gusto.

"So what do you think will happen with the governor's race?" I asked, and the boys discussed the various possibilities of what might happen. They all seemed to agree that Frannie O'Day, a pleasant middle-aged woman who had joined every board, charitable organization and civic association in the state, and used that experience to build a career in the state senate, was probably going to end up in the governor's office.

"We could probably do a lot worse than ole Frannie," Harlan said, popping a potato chip in his mouth. "In fact, she'll probably do a helluva lot better than Preston would've."

A few minutes later, as we were all munching on some of Junior's freshly baked chocolate chip cookies and sipping on some coffee, Billy Church looked at me.

"Say, Julius, I might have a project you can take on," he said.

"Sounds ominous," I said. "Shoot."

"You know Deke Scanlon, right?"

Everyone around the table groaned.

"God didn't make too many bigger pains in the ass than ole Deke," Harlan said, and we all nodded in agreement.

Derrick 'Deke' Scanlon was the scion of one of Little Penwick's oldest families. His forebears had arrived in town in the early 18th century and bought up a big chunk of land in the northern part of town. There was a creek running through the land which the original Scanlons had dammed up so they could build a grist mill using the water running out of the new Scanlon Pond. Later, they built a lumber operation next to the grist mill to create boards for the townspeople to use to build their farms and homes.

Between those two businesses, the Scanlon family became wealthy, at least by Little Penwick standards. Generations of kids went ice skating in the winter on Scanlon Pond, fished and swam there in the summers and attended lavish holiday parties in the Scanlon's big house set back from the road a bit on the Long Highway.

Deke was the last surviving member of that distinguished old family, now in his eighties, and was renowned around Little Penwick as the town grump. I couldn't remember if he had ever married, but I don't think he did, because there were no more Scanlon's after Deke. In addition to being grumpy, he was a notorious skinflint, fought every increase in his property tax valuation and drove a fifteen year old Ford pickup that you could hear coming two miles away. It's a miracle that he didn't fall through the rusty floorboards of that old beater, like Fred Flintstone. But the one time I had pulled him over and ticketed him for being out of inspection, the truck had passed, emissions and all.

The grand old Scanlon place had long since been pulled down, and Deke now lived in a two-room cabin on a small lot overlooking a distant corner of the pond. About ten years earlier, Deke's older brother Frank Scanlon III, who everyone in town called 'Trippy,' had donated several hundred acres of land around Scanlon Pond to the Little Penwick Land Preservation Trust. The Trust, financed by some of the rich summertime residents, along with some grants from the big institutions up in Providence, had bought a lot of land in Little Penwick over the last decade or so, farmlands and forests, beachfront and swampland, hoping to keep it free from modern development, leaving the pristine acerage as it was for generations to come.

The Trust created the Scanlon Pond Recreation Area in this newly donated parcel, and it was one of Little Penwick's most popular recreation sites. Fishermen loved the trout-stocked pond, and the new trails and fishing decks installed here and there around the pond. Hikers and walkers enjoyed the trails winding through the thick woods. And in winter, those trails doubled as cross-country tracks, when we had enough snow. And kids, when the weather was cold enough, could skate and play hockey on the pond, as they had for literally two hundred years.

Deke Scanlon, as the younger brother, had not participated in Trippy's donation and kept title to his own section of land on the north side of the pond. He hated visitors and the police had often been called out to help unwary visitors who had been held up at shotgun point by Deke, who wanted them charged with trespassing.

Scanlon could be counted on to show up at town council meetings to complain about something: visitors leaving litter behind, people being too noisy, kids starting bonfires … there was always something. I knew that Bob Murtha, the almost-permanent council president, had given up trying to keep Deke away from his meetings. He just gave the man five minutes and let him ramble. That was usually enough to satisfy his desire to make himself heard.

"What has Deke done now?" I asked.

Billy chuckled. "Nothing," he said. "At least not yet. As you know, I'm on the board of the Land Trust, and we want to make him an offer on the rest of his land, to keep it wild and undeveloped forever, not to be finalized until he shuffles off his mortal coil. And knowing what an ornery cuss he is, I'm sure that blessed event will be years and years from now."

"Great idea," I said. "Who drew the short straw to get to make that offer to him?"

Billy didn't say anything. He just looked at me and smiled.

"You realize I'm retired now, right?" I said. "I don't get free access to bullet-proof vests anymore. Just walking up his driveway is an invitation to get shot. But to ask him to sell his land? Holy crap. He'd go nuclear."

"He's always said he thinks you were a straight shooter," Billy said. "I think that means he likes you."

"Deke Scanlon doesn't like anyone, including the ice cream man," I said. "I think I'll take a hard pass, thanks anyway."

Billy nodded, as if he had been expecting my reaction.

"Don't blame you," he said. "Deke can be pretty unpleasant. But somebody needs to go talk to him. Maybe you can take Siggi with you. She gets along with everybody."

"Not sure I can justify putting her at risk, too," I said. "But let me talk to her. If she'll go with me, I might do it. Deke's always had that chivalry streak in him."

"Awesome," Billy said. "Thanks, Chief."

"Don't thank me yet," I said darkly. "I'm still a hard pass until Siggi says so."

CHAPTER 7

The next morning, I drove up to Boston. The Honorable Robert L. Cabot had his chambers at the Federal Courthouse on Fan Pier overlooking the waterfront. I had called his clerk and she agreed to squeeze me in for half an hour at the end of his lunch period. Named after a longtime corrupt Congressman from Boston, the towering brick and glass courthouse structure is located on Fan Pier in the Seaport district and casts an impressive shadow of federal power over the waterfront.

Judge Cabot had agreed to give me a half hour or so during his lunch hour, which, like most federal judges, extends for two hours. That gave the Honorable Judge time to actually go have lunch at the Parker House, the Harvard Club or someplace on the waterfront, before my allotted thirty minutes, before he got back to work sending miscreants off to the federal prisons in the afternoon. Trust me, it's nice work if you can get it. And Rob Cabot, the brother of Cynthia Knox, got it. He had to go to St. Paul's School, Harvard, and Yale law, then do a twenty-year stint in a nosebleed law firm way up high in one of Boston's skyscrapers before his lifetime of campaign contributions and his old family name netted him the lifetime appointment to the federal bench. But he persevered.

I paid the forty dollars to the guy in some underground parking garage and made my way through the energetic security at the federal courthouse to reach Judge Cabot's chambers on the ninth floor. His matronly secretary smiled at me, nodded at the comfortable chairs in the waiting area and told me the judge would be right with me. There was Muzak wafting through the speakers, but the table in the waiting area had crisp new copies of three of today's newspapers: the Globe, the New York Times and the Wall Street Journal. I picked up the WSJ, which is probably the last of the classic newspapers still published today. I'm sure they run just as much political crap as anybody else, but for the most part, the reporters still ask a lot of questions to find out why Amalgamated Holdings' quarterly results are good, bad or indifferent, and they state the reason right up there in the first graf. Even if you don't give a rip about Amalgamated Holdings, and I certainly don't, it's refreshing to read actual, well-reported news for a change.

So I was reading a long piece about cattle futures, which did not once mention methane flatulence emissions, when the matronly secretary coughed and said "He'll see you now, Mister Haddock." I carefully refolded the newspaper, smiled at her and went inside his chambers.

Rob Cabot was a round man with a shiny half-bald head, a tonsure of hair clinging to the sides and back of his round head. He wore black-framed half-glasses on the end of his nose. Without his official robe, which hung on a coat rack next to his desk, he looked a little reduced in his crisp white dress shirt and striped rep tie. He stood up, smiled and stuck out his hand.

"Chief Haddock," he said, motioning me to sit down in front of his desk. "I understand you wish to talk about the murder of my brother-in-law. I'm glad to help, if I can. But let's make it quick, shall we? I have a kidnapping case on the docket this afternoon."

"Thank you, your Honor," I said. "I'll be as quick as I can. Wouldn't want to get in the way of dispensing justice."

He gave me a sharp look, part query and part warning not to screw with him, so I got down to it.

"Where were you Tuesday morning?" I said. "From between roughly seven-thirty a.m. until nine?"

"Am I a suspect?" Cabot said, a wry smile on his face.

"Please answer the question," I said. "I don't have much time."

"I was at home," the judge said. "I awaken sometime around seven most mornings, have coffee, read the paper, chat with my wife. I usually arrive here at around ten, which I believe I did that morning. I was hearing cases all day."

"Thank you," I said. "I assume your wife will attest to all that?"

He just looked at me.

"I am interested, your Honor, in the dynamic of the Knox family, from your point of view," I said. "We have been told by several members of the family that you and Preston were not close."

"Never liked the man," Cabot said. "No secret about that. I didn't think he was good enough for my sister. Cynthia's instincts have always been sharp, except for when she decided to marry Preston Knox. I never trusted him, never thought he was a good partner for her. What I heard about him, from others I trust, and what I observed of his behaviors over the years … well, my initial impressions were, unfortunately, born out."

"You mean his women troubles?"

He nodded. "And it wasn't just that he had a hyper-active zipper all these years," he said. "He had a knack for getting involved with exactly the wrong sort of people. Over and over again."

Cabot paused and looked at me. "This conversation is off the record," he said. "And I mean completely off the record. I am providing you with the deepest of background, and will deny I said anything if any of this comes to light. Are we clear?"

I nodded, expecting nothing less from a federal judge. "Of course," I said.

"I told Cynthia from the beginning that she needed to keep a close eye on Preston and his associations," he said. "There were law professors at Dartmouth who spoke to me confidentially about Preston. There were women who came to me in private. There were, umm, officials from law enforcement. The picture they all painted was not a pretty one, at all."

"But he managed to get elected attorney general, and was the favorite to get to be governor," I said. "He was not unsuccessful."

Judge Cabot smiled at me, thinly, without humor. "There is a wide difference between being successful and being an upstanding moral individual," he said. "Preston might have been one, but he was never the other."

"What about his kids?" I asked.

He shrugged. "We would see each other at the occasional holiday gathering," he said. "I thought Preston spoiled his daughter, over-indulged her."

"And the boy?"

He shrugged again. "I liked David," he said. "His teen years have been challenging ones. Cynthia complains about that. But he doesn't seem much different than any other teen these days. All about screen time and mood swings."

Cabot glanced at his watch. My thirty minutes was apparently up. I stood up, thanked him for his time and left.

Out in the outer office, I stopped by the desk of the judge's secretary. I asked her if she could look up the judge's calendar for last Tuesday, the day Knox was killed. She punched a few keys and nodded at the screen.

"He came in after lunch," she said. "Had a case that lasted all afternoon. They adjourned at five-thirty."

"So he wasn't here in the morning?"

"No sir," she said. "After lunch."

"And that afternoon case began at …?"

"Two o'clock sharp," she said. "Judge Cabot is very punctual."

I thanked her and left.

Heading back south, I took I-95 back down to Providence and swung over to the state police headquarters. Upstairs, Davis Ruggerio and Jonah Allen were sitting together in Davis' office. They both looked surprised when I walked in.

"Just got back from talking with Judge Cabot," I said. "He lied to me about where he was that morning." I told them what he had said and what his secretary had told me.

Davis groaned.

"This is getting worse and worse," he said. "First, our leading candidate for governor gets whacked. Then a sitting federal judge lies to us."

"And the judge admitted he never liked Preston," I said. "Thought he wasn't good enough for his sister, Cynthia."

"You sure he wasn't playing hooky?" Jonah said. "Maybe you should check with The Country Club, see if Judge Cabot had a regular tee time or something."

"I can do that," I said. "All we've got right now is that he lied to me. What that means, we don't know yet."

"It seems lying runs in the family," Davis said, tapping a pencil on his desk. "I just got a call from Donovan from the FBI. His agents down in Philly have learned that Little Miss Samantha Knox was also blowing clouds of bullshit gas our way the other day."

"Really?" I said. "Like what?"

"She said she wasn't dating anyone serious," he said. "The agents found that she's had a serious and steady boyfriend for over a year now."

"Anyone we know?"

Davis looked down at his notes.

"Name is Javed Bidwai," he said. "Comes from Calcutta. Or Kolkata, if you want to be politically correct. Father is some big industrialist there, well connected in society and politically. Master Javed has been at Penn four years now, working on his business degree."

"Why is she trying to hide him?" I asked.

Davis shrugged. "We're not sure, but the feds talked to some of her roomies, and they said Samantha has been talking lately about taking a semester or two off so she can go with Javed back to Calcutta and launch an NGO."

I must have looked confused.

"That's a Non-Government Organization," Davis said. "A charity of some kind. They want to help the kids in the slums with education, housing, food and all that stuff."

"I thought she was on a pre-law track," I said.

"She is," Jonah Allen said. "Or was, until this Javed character got his hooks into her. Apparently, she came back up to Barrington about two weeks ago to ask her father if he would agree to this new plan for her life. The roomies told the feds that Samantha came back to school upset. Said she and her Daddy had words. She got a flat no."

"This was two weeks before Preston was killed?"

"Yep."

"Didn't she tell us she hadn't been back home since she left for school in August?"

"Yep."

"Do we know where this Javed guy is right now?"

"Yep," Jonah said with a snarky smile. "As soon as he heard that Preston Knox had been murdered, he caught a flight back to India. Good place to hide, in amongst the two billion people there."

"Well, well, well," I said. "Isn't that interesting?"

"Sure is," Davis nodded. "I've been on the phone all morning with Bill Donovan and the state department down in DC. Trying to arrange for someone to go and find Javed Bidwai and ask him some questions."

"How long is that going to take?" I wondered.

Davis shrugged. "No one can tell me," he said. "It might be a few days. It might be a few months. It's a big country. And they're not usually disposed to helping American law enforcement track down one of theirs."

"So we're thinking Javed came up to Barrington, whacked Daddy Knox for being mean to his little girl, jumped on a plane and vamoosed to India," I said. "That's what we've got here?"

"That's a possible theory of events," Davis said. "We need a little more time and some luck before we can call it that way."

"And now we also have Judge Cabot of Boston," Jonah said. "Who might have driven down early that morning, offed his brother-in-law and made it back to Boston in time for afternoon court."

"And possibly Cynthia Knox, who, according to several people I've talked to, seems to have run out of enthusiasm for her marriage," I said. The other two looked at me funny. "I know, we have nothing to go on with her," I continued. "But you both know that angry spouses are always good suspects in a domestic like this."

Davis Ruggerio held up a thick hand.

"We don't even know if this was a domestic killing," he said. "Coulda been the kid's boyfriend, coulda been the judge, coulda been the wife. Or it coulda been someone else we haven't thought about yet."

"You guys check out that cable TV truck thing?" I asked.

Jonah nodded. "Yeah, that's another one," he said. "Called the cable company. They got no records of any of their trucks on Knox's street that day. Not to say it wasn't there—could have been the technician getting an early start, not calling it in. But I did call the Hayes guy next door and he doesn't remember seeing any white panel van outside that morning. And it certainly wasn't his house getting any cable TV work done."

"So little Davie was either mistaken or he's lying to us too," I said.

The other two nodded and looked pretty glum. We were getting more questions than answers. So far. I stood up.

"Going home," I said. "Haven't seen my honeybun in a while."

CHAPTER 8

I WENT TO have coffee with Gus in the morning at the Commons Cup. He was interested in what we had learned about the murder of Preston Knox.

"So what's it like being a statie?" he asked me, once we had our coffee and muffins, and had greeted Betty, the always frazzled proprietor of the Cup.

"I'm not a statie," I said curtly. "I'm an adviser. Or an appointee. A task forcer. But I'm not one of them. I don't even look good in kinky boots and striped pants."

His eyes twinkled as he looked at me over the rim of his coffee mug.

"OK, Mr. Appointee," he said. "What have you learned so far?"

"Not a hell of a lot," I said. "The Knox family seems riven with issues, though."

"Riven?" he said, eyebrow raised. "What does that mean?"

"Means all of them are spinning tales as fast as they can," I said. "We're trying to toss out the BS and get down to the meat and potatoes."

Gus smiled. "What was it that Russian writer dude said? All happy families are alike, but all unhappy families are riven in their own way. Or should it be 'roved?'"

I chuckled. "I didn't know you were an English major."

"Russian literature," he said. "Everyone in those novels ends up dead in the end. Depressing as hell."

I looked at him. "Well, hate to break this to you on a lovely fall morning, but actually we all end up dead, in the end."

"Which is why we have kids," said the soon-to-be-father. "They live on after us. A form of immortality."

"And here I thought we had kids to score some excellent tax deductions," I said.

I changed the subject. "How's your new crew doing?" I asked. "No problems?"

"They're all doing pretty well," he said. "They all get the job, which is big. Now they just need a few months of doing it, over and over. In the rain. In the snow. Late at night. Before dawn. Weekends. Give them all six more months to get some experience under their belts and I think we'll have three pretty good new cops."

"Until they decide to move up to a bigger department, with more excitement," I said.

Gus shrugged. "I can't do anything about that," he said. "This *is* a pretty small town. I don't expect any of my department to stay here for twenty-five years, like you did."

As if on cue, Janice Anderson, a woman in her seventies who'd lived in Little Penwick for about half that time, came up to our table. She looked at Gus.

"I have a complaint to make, Chief," she said.

"OK, Janice," Gus said. "Complain away."

She looked around. The Cup was about half full this morning.   "Here?" she said.

"Yup," Gus said. "I'm ready, you're here, I'm here. I've had my coffee. What's on your mind?"

"One of you officers was impertinent to me the other day," she said.

"Which one?" Gus asked.

"I don't know," she said. "The black one." She looked around again guiltily, making sure no one was paying too much attention. No one was.

"OK," Gus said, nodding to himself. "You do know we have two new officers in the department who are people of color. Which one was it?"

"How am I supposed to know that?" she exclaimed, throwing her hands out.

"All my officers have a name badge on their uniform," Gus said patiently. "Right above their chest pocket. Pretty easy to read."

"Well, I didn't read it," Janice said, looking flustered. "All I know is that he was black and he was impertinent."

"Can you tell me what happened?" Gus said. He had the patience of Job. I would have told her to go down to the beach and pound some sand.

"Yes," she said, eyes lighting up. "I was down at Petrocelli's Pharmacy getting my pills and I came out of the store and ran right into him. He said "'Scuse me, ma'am.'"

She looked at us as though that was the evidence that would lead directly to the electric chair.

"He said 'Excuse me ma'am?'" Gus repeated.

"That's right."

"I don't see what's impertinent about that," Gus said.

"He called me ma'am," she said.

"And you're not a ma'am?" Gus said. "I gotta say, you look like a ma'am to me."

"Well, yes I am," she said. "But no one calls me that. It's … it's impertinent."

"What day was this?" Gus pressed.

"Let me think," Janice said. "Oh, yes, it was Thursday morning. I had to get a refill on my …"

"Thursday morning," Gus repeated, cutting her off. "If I recall, LaToya was on daytime shift. Was this impertinent officer of yours a woman, Miz Anderson?"

"A woman?" she said, eyes widening. "You have a black woman over there?"

"Why yes, we do," Gus said. "Is that a problem?"

"Well, umm, I don't know," she hesitated. "Have we ever had a black woman in the police in this town?"

"I really don't know," Gus said. "Since we at the police department do not spend a lot of time worrying about each other's skin color. Nor what kind of equipment they carry in their boxer shorts. We just try to hire the best people we can find to protect law and order. Do you have any complaints about law and order in the town that you'd like to register with me, Janice?"

His eyes had narrowed and I could see that little twitch in his jaw that told me he was boiling mad inside. He was pretty good about disguising it, though. He must have learned that serving with the Rangers in the Middle East.

I don't know what Janice had hoped to gain from her little scene. But even she could tell that it had landed with a dull thump.

"No," she said, eyes cast down, face reddening. "Thank you, chief." She made a quick retreat back to her own table, where her husband had his nose buried deep in the morning newspaper.

Gus counted to ten, silently. Then he stood up, and picked up my ticket.

"The town of Little Penwick would be happy to buy your coffee, Dad," he said. "But please watch your step up in Providence. This isn't an ordinary homicide case. There are layers behind layers, and they go all the way up to the governor's office. Just mind your P's and Q's."

I stood up and followed him out of the Cup. It was another gorgeous fall day, clear, sunny and cool.

"Has anyone ever explained what the P's and Q's are that we're supposed to mind?" I said. "Don't think I've ever seen any P's and Q's running around loose."

"Have a nice day, Dad," Gus said, shaking his head and heading for his squad car.

BACK AT MY place, I kicked off my shoes, rummaged around in my desk to find a legal pad and a pen, and went out onto my deck. The sun was warm enough that I could sit at my picnic table, admire the view and enjoy the peace and quiet to think a bit.

Gus' question about progress in the case kept running around in my head. It had been three days since Preston Knox was murdered, so far we had no solid leads and no suspects. That was unusual. Especially in a crime of passion. Someone took a fireplace tool to the head of Preston Knox and applied it with violence until the man was dead. To do that requires a lot of emotion. A cold-blooded contract killer will slit your throat, shoot you in the head, run you over, shove you out the window ... but however he does the deed, he does it quickly, quietly and then bugs out, trying to avoid capture. When the killer picks up a fireplace poker and slams it into your head three or four times, with malice aforethought, it's a crime of passion. A great, overwhelming tide of anger took over that person and tripped his wires. Or hers. It was probably un-planned, spur of the moment. Something Knox had said that morning caused the unknown person to overload, go nutty and pick up the handiest tool he, or she, could find. Pow. Pow. Pow. And he's dead. Then what?

According to the police report, the killer had dropped the fireplace poker and left the house. He, or she, must have been wearing gloves, since there were no fingerprints on the poker, other than those belonging to the family members.

I picked up my phone and called John Richardson, who had been Knox's driver and bodyguard. He didn't pick up, so I left a message, asking him to call me. I needed to hear from him what had been going on in Knox's world just before he was killed. And why Richardson had been given the morning off.

"Hey, mister."

The young, high-pitched, prepubescent voice startled me out of my reverie. I looked over at my fence and the strange kid's head was back, peering at me over the top. Today he was wearing a Sox cap, shading half his face.

"Hey yourself," I said. I waved at him. "Why doncha come on over and sit a spell? I won't bite. Promise."

He looked a little doubtful, but eventually the head disappeared and, moments later, he climbed the stairs of the deck and plopped down on the bench of the table opposite me. He was dressed in a long sleeve T-shirt, blue jeans, and sneakers. His hair was dark and, underneath his baseball cap, looked mostly orderly, if not perfectly combed. I had been right: he looked to be around twelve or thirteen years old, all elbows and knees. Dark eyes and a dark complexion. Maybe Hispanic, but it was hard to tell. Southern European for sure.

I looked at my watch. It was just after 11. School was in session. Without this kid.

I stuck out my hand across the table. "I'm Julius," I said. "I was named after Julius Caesar, who was a Roman emperor about two thousand years ago."

"Really?" the kid said, shaking my hand and quickly letting it go. "I'm Mattie." He thought for a moment or two. "Why did your father name you that? Did he think you'd become an emperor too?"

I laughed. "I don't know," I said. "I really never knew my Dad. He went off to fight in a war when I was about three and was killed in action."

"Really?" Mattie said. "Cool." Then he realized what he had just said. "I didn't mean it's cool your Dad got killed," he said, "I just ..."

"It's OK," I said. "Happened a long time ago. You get used to it after a while."

Mattie's eyes drifted out to sea, taking in the broad sweep of the sea and the collection of rocks and islets just off my beach that they call 'the Rockies.' The tide was coming in and the waves were beginning to crash over some of the lower boulders, covered in lichen and barnacles.

"Anyone ever live on those islands?" he asked.

"Naw," I said. "These ones close to shore are too low. When the tide comes in a few hours from now, a lot of those rocks will be under water. But you see that bigger island way out there next to the lighthouse?"

He followed my arm as I pointed. "Yeah," he said. "There's something on it. Looks like a chimney or something."

"Good eyes," I said. "There used to be this big hotel on that island, about a hundred and fifty years ago. It's called West Island and the resort was a popular fishing club. That's where that chimney looking thing came from. Rich people used to go out there for the striped bass. They'd fish from these wooden platforms built on top of the rocks. Must have been a great place to stay, huh? Look out your window in the morning and see nothing but endless ocean out to the horizon."

"What happened to it?"

"Time," I said. "The fishing club closed down around 1905, because they had fished out all the striped bass. Eventually the resort closed and the hotel building, which was mostly made of wood, began to rot away. A few hurricanes and storms finished the job. Only thing out there now is a bunch of seagulls and those foundation stones you can see."

"I always wanted to live on a deserted island," Mattie said, a little wistfully.

"Like Robinson Crusoe?" I said.

His face reddened a little.

"I don't know who that is," he said.

"Oh," I said. "He was this guy in a book. Written a long time ago. According to the story, Robinson Crusoe was on a boat going across the sea when a storm came up and the boat sank with all hands. But he somehow managed to make it to the shore of this deserted island. The book is about how he managed to live. Built a hut near the beach. Gathered rain water to drink and figured out how to fish and hunt and pick fruits and stuff to live on. Good story. I think I have a copy. Be happy to lend it to you if you want to read it."

"Cool," he said.

"You live around here?" I said.

He made a nodding motion over his shoulder, as if to indicate *over there*. It didn't tell me much.

"How come you're not in school?" I asked next. "It's almost lunchtime."

"Oh," he said, "Today is a teacher training day. We get the day off."

"Cool," I said. Although I figured he was blowing smoke. I didn't care that much—I wasn't in the business of chasing and arresting truants any more. "You hungry? I could make us some sandwiches. Nothing fancy. Maybe some peanut butter and jelly."

"You can cook?" he said with a grin.

I laughed. "Making a couple of peanut butter sandwiches is *not* cooking," I said. "It's just staving off hunger until you cook something later. Doesn't your Dad ever cook?"

He laughed. "*My* Dad?" he said. "Not in a million zillion years. Mom does all of that stuff."

"Whatever," I said. "I'll go make lunch. What do you like to drink? Coke? Milk? Gatorade? Anything?"

"Coke would be cool," he said.

I left him there and went inside. Took a few minutes to throw together some sandwiches, fill a bowl with potato chips and pour Mattie a glass of soda with some ice. I had a deja vu flashback to my own misspent youth, when my mother would make me the same lunch. Before I went back outside, I rummaged through my bookshelves until I found the old hardback copy of *The Adventures of Robinson Crusoe*. It was an old volume, probably had belonged to my grandfather, and was illustrated with full-page paintings by N.C. Wyeth, so even if Mattie didn't want to read the whole thing, he could get the general idea of the story by looking at the great pictures. I carried the book and the lunch back outside on a tray.

Mattie had found my binoculars, sitting in their leather case on a hook on a porch railing, and was peering out at the island where the resort once stood. He had taken off his baseball cap, which got in the way.

"See anything?" I asked as I put the two plates down, put a PBJ on each one, and set the bowl of chips on the table. I put Mattie's soda down and my iced tea.

"Lotta sea gulls," he said, his eyes pressed hard on the eyepieces. "Not much else."

When he turned to look at me, I noticed, for the first time, that he was sporting what looked like a shiner on his left eye. The eye socket was red and bruised looking, and I noticed, looking closely, there was a small cut hidden underneath his eyebrows.

"What happened to your eye?" I said.

He blushed and looked away. "Fell down," he said. "Hit it on a door."

I smiled at him.

"You remember I'm a cop, right?" I said. "Whenever anyone told me that they fell down or hit something on a door, it always meant someone smacked them upside the head. Anyone smack you, Mattie?"

He didn't say anything. He put the binocs up to his face again and looked some more out to sea. Then he came back to the table, put his hat back on, pulling the brim down low, and began to eat his sandwich. I decided to let it ride. For now.

I showed him the book. "If you're into deserted islands, this is the book," I said. "And it's got pictures, too."

Mattie pulled the book around and looked at the cover while he ate. He opened it and glanced at the first few pages.

"What's your Dad do?" I asked. Always the cop.

He finished chewing the chunk of PBJ before he answered.

"He's a truck driver," Mattie said. "Long haul. When he's on a job, he's gone for a week, sometimes longer."

"You got any brothers or sisters?"

He nodded. "Maria is my sister. She's five. Pain in the neck most of the time."

I nodded, eating my own sandwich. "Yeah, sisters can be that way," I said. "But they'll eventually grow out of it and most of them become pretty cool."

He nodded, but looked doubtful that such a thing would ever happen to him.

"Your Mom work?" I thought I was doing pretty good, getting some information out of the kid, a piece at a time.

He nodded. "Papi owns a little store up in Fall River," he said. "Mom goes up to help him on weekends when she can."

"Papi. That's your grandfather?"

He nodded. He was looking at the pictures in the book again.

"Think you can get that book home?" I said. "If you want, I can get a bag or something you can hang over the handlebars."

"Naw," he said. "I can deal." He looked at me. "Thanks for the lunch."

"You're welcome, son," I said. "Any time. But you should be in school. No matter how stupid you think it is, it's important."

He didn't say anything, but kept his eyes on the book. He drained the last of his glass of soda, ice cubes rattling, and stood up, closing the book and picking it up.

"Gotta get goin,'" he said. "I'll bring the book back when I've read it. See ya around."

"Like a donut," I said.

He thought about that, then laughed. He went down the steps, clutching the book, then turned down the walkway and headed around the corner of the house toward the driveway. He stopped and gave me a wave.

I waved back. Seems like I had made a new friend.

CHAPTER 9

Saturday morning, I got up early and made pancakes. And bacon. And coffee. It's the perfect way to start the weekend. Siggi thought so, since she got up earlier than usual, pulled out of bed by the delicious odors wafting out of my kitchen.

She came out of the bedroom looking relaxed and sleepy and sexy all at once, and wrapped her arms around me while I worked at the stove.

"Is it a special occasion?" she whispered against my neck.

"Yes," I said. "It's Saturday, the sun is shining, and I wanted bacon."

"I didn't realize the day of the week mattered when you wanted bacon," she said.

I watched the bacon sizzling carefully. It was at that stage when they can go from golden brown to black and charred in an instant. But not on my watch.

"Also," I said as she poured herself a mug of coffee, "I'm supposed to go see a guy named Deke Scanlon, who has a reputation as something of a grumpy person, and I thought you might go with me."

"Does this have something to do with the Knox case?"

"Nope," I said. "Bill Church asked me to speak with him. The Land Trust of Little Penwick wants him to donate his land to the town."

"That would make anyone grumpy," Siggi said, watching the bacon sizzling in the pan with undisguised interest.

"Yeah," I agreed. "But Deke is the kind of guy that gets unhappy when the wind shifts to the east."

"And you want me to go to see this unhappy person?" she said. "I thought you liked me!"

"I love you more than life itself," I said. "But I think you could help. And there may be lunch at the Roadhouse afterwards."

The bacon was done. I lifted the pieces out of the hot grease and let them rest on a bed of paper towels. Meanwhile, my last three pancakes were ready to flip and cook on the backside for a minute. I had a plate with another dozen or so keeping warm in the oven at low heat.

"I knew there was something going on," Siggi said, smiling at me fondly. "You think you can bribe me with pancakes and bacon?"

"I call it incentive," I said. I took the warm plate out of the oven, spatula-ed the last three on top and carried it over to the table. I put the bacon on another plate, poured myself a cup of joe and went to sit down. "The good part is that if it doesn't work on you, I can still have a big breakfast, which will make me happy."

I had already set the table, so Siggi sat down and put several pancakes on her plate, adding a few strips of bacon on the side. That left about six for me. Happy, happy, happy.

An hour or two later, once we had eaten, cleaned up, showered and dressed, we got in my SUV. We drove up into the center of Little Penwick, north of the beach and east of the river. After the earliest settlers had denuded the landscape of all trees, the second- and third-growth forests had again taken over the land, and the roads were shadowed by the arching limbs and leaves. The leaves were well on their way to their full fall colors, and in the bright sunlight of this beautiful, sunny day, the colors caught the eye and lifted our spirits.

The Long Highway circled around a corner of Scanlon Pond, past the parking lot to the recreation area. There were a couple of cars in there. Hikers, probably, since fishing season was over. A mile or two on, I looked for and found the narrow dirt road that led deep into the woods.

The northern shores of the pond were visible off to our right as my car rumbled over some old wood-planked bridges spanning the small creeks that made their way down toward the pond. The road bent back to the right, towards the pond, and climbed upwards a bit. Scanlon's house was built on a rocky bluff overlooking the length of the pond, facing south southwest. There was a driveway circle in front of his house, and I pulled in and stopped the car. Scanlon's old red pickup, dusty and rusting at the edges, sat in front of his door.

"What a lovely spot," Siggi exclaimed as we got out.

"Unless there's three feet of snow," I said. "Then he's stuck in here for a week."

"That might be romantic," she said, nudging me in the side.

"For you and me, hell yes," I said. "But Deke lives alone. No one to be romantic with, unless you count his dog."

"Ugh," she said.

I knocked on his door. Waited, listening. Couldn't hear anything from inside. I knocked again, a bit louder. Waited. Knocked a third time.

"Geezus Monday," came a voice from inside. "Keep your pants on. I'm coming already."

The door opened and Deke Scanlon peered out at us. He had been a tall man, but bent with age, his shoulders and back arching forward. He still had a pretty good head of hair, but it was glistening white. His facial features were sharp and angled, his gaunt looking hands dotted with brown spots. He was wearing black corduroys, a white collared shirt and a gray sweater. He studied us as we studied him for a few moments.

"Oh," he said finally. "Chief Haddock, isn't it? What do you want?"

"Hello, Deke," I said. "Good to see you again. This is my partner, Siggi." I nodded at her. "Can we come in for a minute? We have something we'd like to to talk about with you."

"Can't we do it right here?" he snapped. "I don't like company."

"We could," I said, nodding. "But I wanted Siggi to see the view from your porch out back. And what we have to talk about might take a few minutes. Be more comfortable if we were all sitting down."

He thought about that while he glared at us, his eyes darting from looking at me, to looking at Siggi, to coming back to me.

He made a kind of huffing noise, turned on his heel and walked into his house. But he left the door open, which I took as a sign that he wanted us to follow. So we did.

Deke Scanlon's house was pretty compact. We walked into an open room with a ceiling open to the beamed, pitched roof. To our left as we entered was a small compact kitchen with a pass-through counter to the dining space. A large stone fireplace climbed the wall to our right, with Deke's throw-covered sofa opposite, and another chair against the wall next to the fireplace. A door beyond the fireplace led into what I expected was his bedroom and bath. There was a black lab sleeping on an oversized doggy bed in front of the empty fireplace. He raised his head when we walked in, looking at us with tired eyes.

Straight ahead a bank of windows looked out on the wooden porch that extended across the back of the house. And beyond was a stunning view of Scanlon Pond, down below the bluff on which the house perched. You could see almost the entire length of the narrow pond, except for the inlets of the pond that extended off to both sides, hidden behind the trees and rocks.

"Wow," Siggi said when she saw the view. "This is amazing."

Deke drew himself upright in pride. "My father built this house back in the Forties," he said. "Used it as a summer camp for many years. I had her winterized back around Eighty-Two and I've lived here ever since."

Siggi sank down on her knees next to the dog and cooed at him. He moved his head over onto her lap and she rubbed his ears. His tail made a thumping sound on his doggy bed. "What's his name?" she asked.

"Old Dog," Deke said, with a slight smile. "That's what he is, that's what I call him."

I was looking at the stuffed pair of ducks, mounted over the mantel as if they were trying to fly away, wings extended. On another wall, a deer head was mounted on a plank, his dark limpid eyes staring at me, as if to ask What the hell am I doing stuck in here? I had no answer for him.

"You bag these critters?" I asked.

Deke saw where I was looking and nodded. "Yep," he said. "I been hunting and fishing this land since I could walk. Know every inch like the back of my hand."

He motioned for us to sit down. I did, on the sofa. Siggi stayed on the floor with the dog. Deke sat down in the adjoining chair. He didn't offer us anything to eat or drink.

"Whaddya want?" he said.

Taking my cue, I got right down to business.

"We're here today to talk about the future," I said.

"I live in the here and now," he said.

"Which is absolutely the right way to live," I said, nodding. "But some day we all gotta shuffle off our mortal coil, and we want to make sure you have made plans to make sure that all this …" I nodded at the windows and the view beyond …" isn't lost or broken up by developers."

"After I'm dead, I don't give a crap what happens," he said. His eyes were narrow and suspicious. "What is it you're trying to say, Chief? Spit it out, sonny boy."

"My friend Billy Church—you know him, right? Church Insurance?—he's on the board of the Little Penwick Land Trust. Now, we all know that you've donated several hundred acres already to the Trust…"

"Wasn't me," Deke snapped. "That was my brother Trippy. He signed over six hundred and forty-two acres just before he died. Nineteen Ninety-Five. He had the cancer."

"Well, that was nice of him," I started. Deke cut me off.

"He did that to spite me," he said. "Instead of passing the Scanlon land on to the last surviving Scanlon, he gave it away to strangers. Something he learned from my Daddy. And look what's happened. People … strangers …walking all over our land. Creating a mess. Paper, plastic, fishing line, used condoms. It's a disgrace."

"I guess he thought he was trying to preserve the natural beauty of the land," I said. "Make it available to all those who loved this pond, who fished and hunted and skated and camped here when they were kids."

Deke looked at me with barely disguised contempt.

"Geez," he said. "You've swallowed that tree hugger crap straight up, haven't ya? Well, I got a different outlook."

"What is that?" Siggi asked, from her position down on the floor next to the dog. He looked at her, hard at first. Then his eyes softened a bit.

"This is Scanlon land," he said, motioning out the bank of windows at the scene below. "My family came here in 1673 and settled it. We dammed up the creek and made a sawmill and a grist mill, so people could live. All the early houses around the village green, even the church itself … all built with lumber produced by the Scanlon sawmill. Two hundred years ago, you could see the ocean from this spot. Those mills kept my forebears alive for fifteen generations. I'm the sixteenth. And last."

"1673?" Siggi said. "That is amazing. It must have been virgin forest way back then, wild and wonderful."

"Yes, missy, it was," Deke said, nodding at her approvingly. "The Indians still lived here then, the Pocasset clan of the Wampanoag tribe. But two years later, they started the King Phillip's War. Hundreds of settlers were killed. Not so many around here, but all across New England. Different times. Hard times."

He got out his chair with a groan and picked something off the mantel. He showed it to Siggi.

"These are arrowheads I found myself," he said. "Had the Haffenreffer Museum look at 'em. They think these are fourteenth century. Two hundred years before Miles Standish and those assholes arrived in Plymouth. Found 'em right here on my own land."

"Wow," she said, gazing at them. "That's amazing."

"Well, that's the point, isn't it?" I said. Deke scowled at me. "You're the last of your kind. I'd think you'd want to leave something behind for people to remember you by. Like the rest of the Scanlon land up here. Something for people to enjoy for years to come, in its natural state, thanking you for your generosity."

He made a dismissive sound. *Pshaw.*

"If you don't do anything, it's likely the town will take this land over once you've gone," I said. "They'll just sell to the highest bidder. Probably some real estate sharpie from upstate, or even Boston'll come down here and start building roads and subdivisions and fancy big houses. That'd be a hell of a thing, Deke, to let that happen."

"Well then," he said, "You'll have to stop them from doing that, after I'm gone."

"I won't be able to," I said. "Won't be up to me. There are laws and the town will follow the law."

Deke stared at me for a moment or two. "Nobody will touch this land as long as I'm alive," he said. "If I give it to the Land Trust, they'll have hikers and cross country skiers and fishermen and boaters and everyone you can think of prancing across my land. My land, Chief. Since 1673."

He shook his head, a little angrily now. "No," he said. "I'm not doing it. That's final." He stood up. "I gotta pee," he said. He stalked through the doorway that led back to his bedroom, leaving us wondering what he expected us to do.

Siggi got up and began to look at some of the other items Deke had placed on his mantel. There were some old family photos and other mementos there. I stared out the window, admiring the view again. Billy Church will be disappointed, I thought, but at least I tried.

Deke came back into the room, zipping up his fly.

"You people still here?" he said gruffly. "Don't take 'no' for an answer, do ya?"

I stood up. "We'll go, Deke," I said. "Thanks for hearing us out. Frankly, I agree with you for the most part. I wouldn't want to give up my land. I might leave it to someone I know, or a member of the family, but I'd hate to see it go to strangers."

Scanlon looked at me. I think he was trying to decide if I was telling the truth or blowing some hot air up his hindquarters. Siggi went over to him and kissed him on the cheek.

"It was very nice to have met you," she said. "And Old Dog, too."

He blushed. Probably been years since a woman did that to him.

"Right," he said. We left him standing there, alone in his cabin in the woods.

CHAPTER 10

The Patriots were locked in a defensive battle with Cleveland on Sunday afternoon when there was a loud knock on my front door, the one facing the street. Nobody ever comes to my front door. Friends and family know to walk between the house and the garage and come around to the back, up the three stairs to the deck and knock on the back door. Even our delivery guys have been trained. We used to get some foot traffic on Halloween at the front door, but that died away over the last five or ten years. Little kids don't trick or treat anymore in the neighborhoods. Only the smart-ass teens, who think they're immortal, do.

Siggi, who had been peacefully knitting in her chair, started to put her stuff down to go see who it was.

"I'll get it," I said, standing up. "Probably the Jehovah's. They haven't been out this way in about a year now."

When I opened the door —the hinges squeaked loudly in protest since they hadn't been disturbed in months — I found a short, swarthy, dark skinned man standing there, with a paper bag in his hand.

"Help you?" I said.

"You that police chief?" the man said. His voice was accented. Hispanic. But I'm not good enough at accents to identify country of origin.

"I'm Julius Haddock," I said. "I was the chief of police for twenty-six years in this town. Now I'm retired. What can I do for you, sir?"

He held out the hand that was holding the bag. It was a grocery store paper bag, the kind they use when you tell them 'paper' instead of 'plastic.' There was something heavy and bulky inside. I opened it up and saw my copy of The Adventures of Robinson Crusoe. I looked up at him.

"You're Mattie's Dad," I said. I stood back. "Would you like to come in?" I felt Siggi come up behind me.

"No," he said. "I don wan you givin' my boy books," he said. "He needs books, I get him. OK?" He leveled his eyes at me, challenging me to disagree.

"Sure, I understand," I said. "Didn't mean to cause any problems. Mattie stopped by here a few days ago and we were talking, and he mentioned he liked desert islands. So I thought of this book and asked if he wanted to read it, take it home with him. It's a classic, you know. Daniel Defoe wrote it."

"I don' care about that," the man said. "I bring this back to you. No more books. No more talk. Boy go to school. Go home and help his mother. You got that?"

I could now smell the alcohol on his breath. The more he talked, the stronger the odor was. He was being quite unpleasant, but I understood that it was the booze talking, so I let it be.

"Of course, sir," I said. "I understand perfectly. You should be proud of Mattie. He's a good kid. Polite. Thoughtful. Very smart. He's a credit to you and your wife."

"I know nothin' 'bout all that," he said. "Just keep away from my boy. I don' care you police or not. I don wan you near the boy. You got?"

"I got," I said and slammed the door in the man's face. The heavy door made a satisfactory loud noise. Siggi, standing behind me, jumped. I silently counted to three and, as expected, he began pounding on the door.

"Hey, mothafuck," he yelled. "You can no disrespect Hector Gonzales, you son'a beetch."

I flung the door open again and took two steps forward, grabbing him by the shoulders. I put my face right up close to his.

"Your son, sir, is very well behaved," I said, keeping my voice low and, I hoped, threatening. "He is polite. He is friendly. But your behavior is quite rude. You've got about one minute to get your ass off my property before I tell my partner here …" and I nodded back at Siggi who was standing in the doorway watching with wide eyes … "to go get her gun and shoot your ass. Now git."

I turned him around, put my foot across his buttocks and gave him a helping nudge towards the street. He tried to keep his feet but, with the booze flowing around inside, failed, and went to his knees on the grass of my small patch of front lawn. He quickly jumped to his feet, spun around and stared at me, his face now red and splotchy with rage. His hands were clenched tightly into fists. I waited for him to make the first move. I was fairly confident that, in his inebriated condition, I could handle him.

"Senor!" Siggi called out sharply behind me. "Parar! Solo ve antes de que haya problemas!"

I didn't know exactly what she said, but it seemed to work. He glared at me for another second or two, turned and spat angrily on my lawn, then walked away.

We watched him go. There was a gray pickup out on the street. He climbed into it and drove away, leaving a cloud of smoke in his wake. I thought I heard him shout something as he drove away.

"Well," I said when he was gone. "He was nice. What did you tell him?"

"Just to leave before he got into trouble," Siggi said. "Do you think he'll go home and take it out on Mattie?"

That thought had crossed my mind as well.

"Hope not," I said. "Because otherwise I'll have to get involved."

"You and me both," Siggi said.

She led me back inside and closed the front door. I put Robinson Crusoe back on the bookshelf in the living room. The Pats and the Browns were still tied up. My stomach was twisted in knots. I went looking for another beer.

EARLY THE NEXT morning, I drove back up to Providence. I was beginning to appreciate the stress this daily commute caused for the road warriors who made this drive every day. Even at six in the morning, traffic was heavy. Even with a travel mug that Siggi had filled with hot coffee, I was dragging.

I had two reasons to make the drive today. Davis Ruggerio had texted me to say he had arranged a Skype interview with Jevan Bidwai, Samantha's UPenn friend, who was still in India among the teeming hordes. But he had apparently heard that we wanted to talk to him.

And that afternoon was the funeral for Attorney General Preston Knox. Because he was an elected state officer, the State Capitol had been reserved for the occasion, and all state employees given the day off to mourn. I had packed my formal police uniform in the back of the car, after Siggi had spent an hour ironing everything.

When I got to state police HQ, Davis was setting up a TV monitor, plugging it into his laptop. He logged onto the app and tested the camera and the sound.

"Is there a way to get this thing to record the call?" he asked me.

"You're asking me?" I said. "I'm a tech dinosaur. I use my phone mostly for making calls. Though there is an app I found for keeping a grocery list. That's kinda handy."

He smiled and looked at his watch.

"Don't have time to call in the department's tech nerds," he said. "It's almost showtime. I'll have to go analog." He took out his pocket tape recorder and clicked it on to make sure it had juice.

At the top of the hour, he punched a few buttons on his laptop. We could hear some techie whirrs and groans and then a young man appeared on the screen.

"Hello? … Hello?" the young man said. "Can you hear me?"

"Are you Jevan Bidwai?" Davis said.

"Yes I am."

Davis introduced himself and me. Said that the call was being recorded.

"Mr. Bidwai," he started, "We are interested in your relationship with Samantha Knox, and more importantly, with any interactions you may have had with the late Mr. Knox."

"Yes, I see," the young man said. "I know Sam … Ms. Knox … from Penn, of course. I have only met her father once."

"Were you and Ms. Knox involved in a relationship, Mr. Bidwai?" I asked.

"Do you mean sexual?" he said. "No. Not at all."

"We have information that implies that you two were," I said.

He shook his head, violently.

"No, no, That is incorrect. We were, and are, just friends."

"We have been told that you and Ms. Knox had been making plans to set up an NGO there in India," Ruggerio said. "And that she was planning to move to India to work with you on that project."

"Yes, that is true," the young man said. "We had been discussing this for many months. We want to start with a food kitchen for the hungry, and then take those who come to eat and try to get them into education of some kind. Or job training. In that way, we give them the tools to lift themselves out of poverty. Samantha said her father could help us find private financing, grant money and the like for our idea. We went to Providence to meet with him in September."

"How did that go?" I asked.

He smiled, sadly.

"Not good at all," he said. "Mr. Knox was very busy, of course. He is …was running for governor of that state. But we were able to have lunch with him. He told us very plainly that he would not help us."

"Did he say why?"

"No," Bidwai said. "But the reasons were obvious, at least to me. He did not like me. I am not an American. I speak with an accent. And, most of all, my skin is of the wrong color. And he, like you, believed that Sam and I were intimate friends, which we are not."

"So you came up here to get help in raising funds for your charitable organization, and Knox basically threw you out," I said.

He nodded. "Yes, yes, this is so."

"Mr. Bidwai," Davis said. "We noticed that you left the United States rather rapidly, the day after Mr. Knox was murdered. Can you tell us why?"

"Of course," he said. "It is Diwali, our holiday. We celebrate light, the victory of righteousness and the lifting of spiritual darkness. It is one of our most important holidays and we all try to be with our families."

Davis and I looked at each other. It didn't sound like Jevan and Samantha had a secret plot to murder Knox and abscond to India. And it was beginning to sound like Sam's roommates at Penn had some hyperactive imaginations about what was going on between the two. At least, if what Bidwai was telling us was actually true.

"Are you planning to return to the United States?" Davis asked.

"Yes, of course," he said. "I must catch up on the classes I missed before the exams at the end of the semester. I should be back in Philadelphia by the end of the month."

"We may need to speak to you again at that time," Davis said.

"Yes, of course," Jevan said. "I will do anything I can to help Sam. She is a wonderful person."

Ruggerio ended the call. Then exhaled, loudly.

"Crap," he said. "I was certain this was going to be something."

"Still, Samantha lied to us," I said. "Said she hadn't been home since she went back to school in August. Wonder why she did that?"

Davis shrugged. "Dunno," he said. "We'll get her back in and ask her."

"Where's Jonah today?"

"He went up to Providence College with a female trooper to interview the two young women that are alleged to have been noodling with the AG during the campaign."

I winced. "I told Betsey Levine from the campaign that we'd be gentle with them," I said. "Hope he doesn't bring out the thumb screws."

"That's why I sent the female trooper with him," Davis said. "Told him to let her lead on the interviews. He's supposed to listen in and maybe ask a follow-up." He looked at me. "He's an excellent detective, Julius. Knows his stuff."

I held my hands out wide in protest.

"I don't doubt that for a moment," I said. "Nothing I've seen during this investigation tells me otherwise. I think he's more upset that I'm on the team than the other way around."

He nodded, "Yeah, that's probably true," he said. "But he's also been around the block once or twice. He knows that the politicians are always sticking their noses into our business. None of us like it, but there's really nothing we can do, except our jobs."

I nodded. He was right.

CHAPTER 11

At noon, we left for the Capitol. Because Knox had been the chief law enforcement officer of the state, every police department in the 31 towns and cities sent a detachment of officers to attend the funeral, each dressed in their finest dress uniforms. Gus had detailed Jessica Martin, his second in command, and Cassie Williams, one of his newbie officers, to represent the town of Little Penwick.

There was a sea of blue in the marble rotunda and outside along the walkways leading to the dome, pants legs highlighted with red and gold stripes, shoes and boots polished to a reflective sheen, and acres of service ribbons splashed across uniform breasts. Police cars lined both sides of the streets all around the Capitol building. The state police band was playing mournful dirges, giving way to bagpipers, fifers and the beating of muffled drums. The local TV stations were broadcasting the events live to the entire state, announcers speaking in hushed tones while they described the events.

The police detachments lined up outside the entrance and stood at unmoving attention as Knox's casket was slowly carried inside the rotunda and placed on its bier in the center of the hall. The ecumenical funeral service was shared between the archbishop of the Rhode Island diocese, the presiding bishop of the Episcopal diocese, and representatives of several other faiths and denominations. State and US flags were displayed everywhere.

The "I Know A Guy" state had bestowed upon me the honor of a seat inside the rotunda, even if I was seated way at the back. Davis and Jonah flanked me on the row of folding chairs.

I turned to Ruggerio on my left. "Good turnout," I whispered. "You surprised?"

He just winked at me. He knew that the real number of people who were actually sad about Preston Knox's passing could have fit in one of the smaller private dining rooms down the street at the Capital City Grille.

We watched as Cynthia Knox, the bereaved widow, was escorted into the rotunda by the Lieutenant Governor and seated up in front, next to the casket of her husband.

"They finally found a job for him," whispered Jonah Allen on my right, as we watched. "Widow escort. About his speed."

I smiled at him. Mocking our elected officials is the State Sport in Rhode Island.

The service began, with hymns and scriptural readings, so I mentally tuned out and went back to thinking about the case. I knew Davis and the other brass of the state police must be sweating bullets by now. It had been almost a week since Knox's murder and if they didn't find the perpetrator pretty fast, the media would start going nutsy. They could maybe delay the public blowback until after elections in a couple of weeks, but not for long after.

Cara Romero, the outgoing governor, stood up to deliver the eulogy. It was a short speech, but larded with the usual platitudes. Which was to be expected. What could you really say about Preston Knox? That he was a lifelong grifter, always open to a good bribe, who couldn't keep his zipper up for more than a week or two? The governor told us nothing about that Preston Knox, but instead created a doppelganger who was concerned about his fellow man, devoted to his wife and children and always served the best interests of his state.

We all followed the late AG out to the grassy front lawns, stood at attention while they fired the twenty-one gun salute, and watched in hushed silence while they loaded Preston back into a polished black hearse. They had kept quiet the news that his body was destined for a far corner of the Cabot family plot at the Mount Auburn Cemetery in Cambridge. It seemed somewhat disrespectful that our attorney general and governor-in-waiting would choose to spend eternity resting in the Commonwealth of Massachusetts, of all places. I suspected his widow, Cynthia, just wanted to make sure she knew where he was, for a change.

Funeral over, most of us stood around in groups on the sunny lawn of the Capitol, meeting and greeting old friends. And Rhode Island is a small enough state that everyone knows each other. Several of the other chiefs in the state came over to speak to me. I smiled at them all and, instead of asking all of them where they had been when Knox had railroaded me into jail a year ago, I kept my thoughts to myself. Out of respect to the dead, of course.

I spotted John Richardson, standing with some other state police officers, all dressed in their best Canadian Mountie uniforms: all boots, straps and creased Stetsons. I made my way over and caught his eye. He said something to one of the other staties and came to meet me in the shade of a plane maple tree, its leaves turned a bright, cheerful yellow.

"Chief Haddock," he said, nodding to me.

"How you doing, John?" I said.

He shrugged. What can you say? Your job is to drive a guy around the state and make sure no one attacks him. And then one day, someone does and he's gone. Kind of the ultimate rug-pull.

"How long were you with Knox?"

He looked off down the hill, across the park next to the train station and on into downtown.

"Three and a half years," he said. "Long time."

"You got any idea who did it?"

He shook his head. "Not really," he said. "Over the years, there were a few knuckleheads, guys who made some threatening remarks. I made a list. I think Jonah has already checked them all out. None of them were anywhere near Barrington last week."

"Knox was tight with some of the Family," I said. "Did he get on someone's bad side?"

Richardson shook his head. "Not that I know," he said. "Preston was always a bit cavalier about working with those guys. Said they needed him more than he needed them. He thought that was his insurance policy."

"You think the premium came due?"

He looked at me and shook his head. "Giancarlo and those guys knew that if they tried taking him out, a shitstorm of Biblical proportions would come down on them," he said. "There are unwritten rules. Long as everyone knows the deal and keeps their mouths shut, they can do business. Knox knew the rules."

"Yeah, I don't like those guys for this," I said. "It looks like someone just popped a nutty. If this thing had happened over on Canal Street, you'd be looking for a wino or a druggie who just snapped."

"But there ain't that many winos and druggies walking the streets of Barrington," John said. "Much less getting inside the house of the attorney general."

"You knew about the two chicks from the campaign he was bumping, right?"

He looked at me, surprised.

"How did you k—"

I smiled. "I'm a cop," I said. "I might be a retired one, but I'm still a cop."

He shook his head, probably wondering what happened to keeping the details of this case confidential. But he also knew that in Rhode Island, there aren't many secrets. Everybody tends to know everyone else's business.

"In that job I had, you have to make a lot of judgment calls," he said. "The protectee is entitled to have a private life.

I mean, if I saw him smoking crack or robbing a bank, I would probably step in and say something. The law's the law, right?" He looked at me for confirmation. I nodded.

"But seducing girls is not illegal," he continued. "It might be unprofessional. It might be immoral, even though both those girls are over the age of legal consent. It might be something that makes you kinda mad." He looked at me again, his eyes searching mine for understanding. "I mean, I have a daughter. She's twelve. Going on twenty-five. The idea of her being with someone like Knox." He stopped. And shuddered. He didn't need to continue. I understood.

"So you have to give 'em some room," he said. "Look away, sometimes. Doesn't sit well. But he's got a right to make his own choices, even if those choices aren't ones I would make. My job was to drive the man and keep him safe to do his job."

"Tell me about his family," I said.

He moved his shoulders as if he was getting stiff. He motioned that he wanted to walk, back up towards the marble steps of the Capitol. I walked with him.

"His wife, Cynthia, had mostly checked out," he said. "She spent most of her time up in Boston. They made some kind of agreement that she would help him with the campaign … showing up for events and parties … and then afterwards, they were probably going to officially separate."

"You think she decided to make the separation permanent?" I asked.

He smiled. "Cyn? Naw. She comes from rich folk. She just wanted to go back to them. I don't think Cynthia ever liked living in Rhode Island." He shrugged. "Different strokes, right?"

"I guess," I said. "Any of Cynthia's relatives might want to come down here and remove Preston from the family tree?"

"Her people are hedge fund managers, university professors, raise money for charitable organizations," he said. "They know more about trust funds and lattes than clipping somebody. Very doubtful."

"What about the kids?"

"Sammy's a good kid," he said, smiling. "Sweet girl. Really good at dealing with people. She'll be the politician Preston never could be. Smart, pretty, aware of what's going on around her. I liked her. A lot."

"And the son?"

"David has always been an awkward kid," he said. "He's all elbows and knees and messy hair and pimples. Still growing out, y'know?" He looked at me. I understood, having once been a nerd myself.

"Unlike his sister, he's never been comfortable in the public eye," John continued. "His folks tried to keep him in the background. And he's always been a Momma's boy. But then, Samantha was always the apple of her Daddy's eye."

"How's he doing in school?" I asked.

"Unlike his sister, he's always struggled," he said. "Lately, he's been playing on the golf team at Barrington High. Thinks he's gonna be the next Tiger Woods."

I chuckled. "I remember when we were all looking for the next Jack Nicklaus," I said. "Now it's the next Tiger Woods."

"And ain't nobody ever gon' be as good as Tiger," John said.

Richardson caught sight of some other staties in a group at the side of the building. He turned to me.

"I gotta go, Chief," he said. "Good to see you again."

"Same here, John," I said. "Thanks for the info."

We shook hands, and he marched off.

CHAPTER 12

I was puttering around at home Tuesday morning when I heard the UPS truck pull into my driveway. Javier, the driver on our route, came around to the back door and knocked. He handed me a thick envelope sealed with official-looking tape.

"From the state police," he said. "You're not in trouble, are ya Chief?"

"Hope not, Javy," I said, taking the envelope from him. "You got time for a coffee? I just made a fresh pot."

"That'd be bueno, chief," he said. "Miss Siggi around today?"

I shook my head. "They're a nurse or two short at the doc shop," I said. "She's been pulling in some extra shifts."

"Well, give her my best," he said, pulling off his fingerless gloves and sitting down at my table. I poured us each a cup of joe, put out some cookies and sat down with him. Javier was a hard-working guy, always polite and friendly. Siggi and I always liked talking with him when he brought us packages from Amazon and other stuff.

"How's the wife and kids?" I asked as we sipped.

"Muy bueno," he said. "Jackie's in sixth grade this year and Hugo is on the football team." Javier lived over in Fall River, an aging post-industrial city now home to thousands of immigrant families.

I opened the envelope. It contained a few more reports from the investigation for me to oversee. I stuffed them back in the envelope and tossed it aside.

"Looks important," Javy said.

I shrugged. "I'm working with the state police on the Knox murder case," I said. "So far, they're better at generating reports than they are at catching somebody."

He whistled softly. "Yeah, that's something, isn't it? Guy running for governor gets whacked in his own home. What a world, eh?"

"Sure is," I said. Then I thought of something. "Say, Javy, do you know a family lives somewhere near here, with a twelve, thirteen year old kid named Mattie? He's got a younger sister and his Dad is a long haul trucker. Ring any bells?"

Javier scratched his head, thinking. Then he brightened and snapped his fingers.

"Yeah," he said. "They live off Maple, in one of those apartments. What's it called? Colonial Acres or something? The name is ... wait a sec ... Gonzales! Hector and Marta Gonzales. I know they have a couple kids. I've seen 'em when I deliver there."

Javier drained his cup and grabbed another cookie for the road.

"Thanks for the coffee, chief," he said. "I'll see ya next time."

"I'll be here," I said, "Unless I'm not," and Javy took off.

Now that I had sleuthed out a name for my mystery friend, I went into action. I called Francine Reilly, the school secretary at the Boxford Elementary School. Hilda Jane Boxford had been a highly respected educator back in the Gilded Age, and she had single-handedly dragged Little Penwick's local school into the age of enlightenment. The kids in town had, before Hilda Jane, crowded into a one-room schoolhouse next to a swamp, and by 1880, that was becoming unworkable.

She had been appointed schoolmistress and immediately began demanding the town of Little Penwick appropriate the money required to build a new school building. Like town councils before and since, they resisted and fought and complained … and eventually put up the money. The new school was built overlooking the town green, a couple doors down from City Hall, and when Miss Boxford eventually kicked the bucket, the grateful town named the school in her honor.

Franny had been working at the school for more than twenty years, and she knew everything there was to know about every kid who passed through the glass doors at the front of the stone-facade building. She and I were old friends.

"Julius Caesar Haddock," she exclaimed when she came on the line. Franny was one of the few people in town who knew my middle name, one that I shared with my son, Augustus. "I have not seen nor talked to you in ages! What have you been up to?"

"Nothing much, Franny," I said. "Lost my job, went to jail, got out, semi-retired and I'm now working as a private investigator."

"Oh, I knew all that stuff," she said, laughing. Franny loved to laugh. "How is the lovely Siggi? Is she taking good care of you?"

"Better than I deserve," I said. "How's Artie?" That was Franny's husband. He pretty much ran the town's public works department.

"He's pretty much the same he ever was," she said. "Long as he gets dinner and a cold beer, he's a pussycat." She laughed again. "What can I do for you?"

"I'm trying to find a kid, I think his name is Matt Gonzales," I said. "I think the family lives in those apartments off Maple Road."

"Oh, yeah," Franny said. "Mattie and Maria. He's in fourth grade. Maria is pre-K. Why are you asking?"

"Curiosity, mostly," I said. "He's stopped by my house a couple times recently. Seems to be a nice kid."

"But?" Franny was wise to my ways after all these years.

"Well, he visited me during school hours," I said. "I'm hoping he's not in any trouble at school. Or at home."

"Uh-huh," she said. I could hear her typing something on her keyboard. "Yes," she said, "Mattias Gonzales. He's been absent six times so far this year."

"In what?" I said, "About six weeks of school so far?"

"That's right," she said. "And I'm just seeing here that he was absent again yesterday. I'm seeing some red flags here."

"What do you do about that?"

"I called his mother a few weeks ago," Frannie said. "She seems nice. She told me she has sometimes needed Mattie to stay home and watch over his sister, so Mom can go work at the family store in Fall River. We don't get too much of that anymore. That's real old school. Most people these days arrange some kind of childcare."

"And the two times he stopped by my house, there was no Maria," I said. "Do you think there's trouble at home? Last time he was here, it looked like he had a shiner on one eye. What do we know about his father?"

"I really don't know," Franny said. "My understanding is that he works as a long-haul trucker for a shipping company based in Seekonk. I don't think Mr. Gonzales has ever made an appearance here at school. It's the mother who comes to teacher conferences and the like. By the way, Mattias is an excellent student, when he's here. He gets good marks and is not one of our behavioral problems. His teachers like him. But you are right … this absenteeism is unusual. And what you tell me about his shiner is worrisome. Let me look into it a little more."

"Don't be fingering me, Franny," I said. "Like I said, he seems to be a good kid. We talk about stuff. I don't want him to think I turned him in or anything."

"Not to worry, chief," she said. "I'll do it on the Q.T."

"Thanks, Fran," I said. "You're the best."

"I know that, and you know that," Franny said. "I just wish the superintendent knew that. I need a raise."

This time I laughed and we rang off.

CHAPTER 13

Davis Ruggerio called a Task Force meeting the next morning, bright and early, so I battled the morning commuters to get to Providence, thinking for the thousandth time that I would rather give myself a root canal than have to do this every day.

In a large conference room at state police HQ, Davis, Jonah Allen and I sat at the head of the table and about a dozen others — both uniformed troopers and plainclothes detectives — took seats in front of us.

Ruggerio recapped our progress to date, which didn't take very long, then asked Jonah for any new updates on the case.

"I went to Providence College yesterday to speak with two individuals said to have been intimately involved with Preston Knox during his campaign," Jonah said, looking at his notes. "Because these were young women, and because of the sensitivity of the subject matter, I took Trooper Sarah Wilcox with me to conduct the interviews."

He looked up and nodded at Wilcox, who was sitting near the front. She smiled at us. She was dressed today in civilian clothes, pants and a sweater top. She was young, in her thirties, with long brown hair.

"Subject A was embarrassed and contrite," Allen continued. "She seemed most concerned that her father never found out about her activity with the victim. Trooper Wilcox assured her that, unless her testimony is required in court at some future date, that her records will be kept confidential."

I looked at the printed case notes that had been handed to me that morning. Subject A was identified as Angie Sagassian, the co-ed Betsey Levine had described to me as 'a looker' whom she had put into the communications effort of the campaign.

"Subject A had left the campaign at the beginning of September to return to school," Jonah continued. "She says she had not seen or spoken with Preston Knox since she left. It is our opinion that she is not connected with the crime."

He shuffled his papers.

"Subject B had a somewhat different attitude when we questioned her," he said. "She was more defiant and angry at us for asking questions about her personal life." He paused at looked up at the room. "I believe I heard phrases like 'defund the police,' 'none of your effing business' and 'I hope the next governor fires the lot of you.'"

There were some titters and noise in the room. Davis Ruggerio looked up and the room fell silent again. I looked at my case notes and saw that Subject B was Camilla DeRosa. I remembered Levine telling me that the two girls were political science majors, which is no doubt where Camilla's attitude toward law enforcement came from.

"Subject B refused to answer when she had last seen or spoken to Preston Knox," Jonah continued. "Trooper Wilcox and I immediately filed a subpoena to get her phone records, which should be available to us in a day or two."

"Okay," Davis said. "Check those records when you get them, see when she last talked to our vic."

"See if you can get an audio," someone said from the back. "Might be hot."

There were more titters in the room, again squelched when Ruggerio gave them the stare.

"What else?" Ruggerio said when the room was quiet again.

I raised my hand. "I'm going to pay a visit to Barrington High," I said. "See if Davie Knox has any problems, academic or behavioral. Maybe talk to some of his teachers, see what they think of the kid. And I want to speak with this Kuhn kid, his best friend, see what he thinks."

"You're still focused on the kid?" Jonah Allen sat back, his voice dripping with sarcasm. "Everything we know about him says he's just a nerdy teenager with angst issues because Daddy was famous. I don't get why you're still looking at him."

"He was the last person, that we know about, to see his father alive," I said. "And he's told us a few whoppers along the way. I don't know if he's the killer. In fact, I'm pretty doubtful that he is. But he's a stone left unturned. So I'm going to go over to the high school and kick a few rocks. See what crawls out."

Davis Ruggerio nodded.

"Okay," he said. "I get that. Just be careful, Julius. There are a lot of connected kids at that school. You step on the wrong toe, it'll blow back on the rest of us. Just a word to the wise."

I was going to remind Davis, and everyone else, that this was a murder investigation, and stepping on toes was what we were supposed to do to get to the truth and find the killer. But I kept my peace. Siggi would have been proud of me picking my spots and not being the usual pain in the butt.

"Anything else?" Davis said to the room.

Nobody responded at first. Then a hand was raised. A woman, dressed in a nice business suit, was standing against the wall to my right.

"Chief Ruggerio," the woman said. "We're starting to get some calls in the Communications Department from the press. It's been a few days since you last spoke to them on the record, and it might be a good idea to do a press conference soon. I'm getting the sense that they're about to start asking why we haven't arrested anyone yet."

"The investigation continues," Davis intoned in his best official-cop stentorian voice. "When we have new information, we will let the public know."

"I understand, chief, I really do," the woman said, her face reddened a little. "But we don't want to face a viral uprising in the press. It would be helpful if you could tell them one or two things that you've learned so far. Keep them informed and on our side."

"As opposed to taking the side of the killer?" he retorted.

"No, chief," she tried again, face a little redder. "We just want them to stay in their lane. And to do that, we have to give them something every now and then."

Davis looked at the woman from comms for a beat or two, then nodded.

"You're right," he said. "I'll have my assistant contact you, set something up this week."

"Thank you, chief," she said.

"If that's all, we'll reconvene in a few days," Ruggerio said and stood up. The room quickly emptied as everyone went back to work.

I followed Davis and Jonah down the hall towards Ruggerio's office. When we pushed through the doors of the Major Crime Unit, a young woman came rushing up.

"Chief," she said, "Charles Elkington is waiting in your office with Cynthia Knox. They got here twenty minutes ago. He wouldn't tell me what they wanted."

Davis sighed. "Okay, Jen, thanks." He turned to look at Jonah and me. "Let's go see what fresh hell awaits."

Cynthia Knox and her attorney were sitting in Ruggerio's guest chairs in front of his desk. Both were, as usual, elegantly turned out. Elkington had his leather briefcase on his lap. Cynthia's face looked a little flushed to me. Jonah and I stood against the wall.

Davis shook both of their hands before walking around his desk and sitting down. He put the folders he was carrying down, arranged the edges and looked at Elkington.

"Good morning, counselor," he said. "What brings you here today?"

Elkington opened his briefcase, rooted around inside it for a moment and withdrew a document. He took another moment to study it, as if he had never seen it before. He glanced at Cynthia Knox to his left, who nodded. Elkington turned the sheet around so that Davis could read it and placed it on the desk in front of him. Ruggerio picked it up and studied it in silence.

"This is our proffer of acknowledgment of accountability by my client in the matter currently under investigation by your department," Elkington said. "It is made fully, freely and without coercion or the influence of any other."

Davis Ruggerio finished reading the document — it was one page — then sat back in his chair and looked across his desk at Elkington and Cynthia.

"You are confessing to the murder of Preston Knox?" he said, his voice flat.

"She is," the lawyer said.

"I want to hear it from her, counselor," Davis said.

"I am," Cynthia Knox said. "I did it."

"I thought you were in Boston with the household staff?" Jonah Allen chimed in next to me.

"I — I came back home early that morning," Cynthia said, turning to look at us against the wall. "It was after Davie had left for school. Preston was there. Something snapped inside me. I don't know what, I don't know why. Our marriage had been entirely fictional for years. I walked by the fireplace, saw the poker in the stand on the hearth, picked it up and smashed Preston in the head with it."

"How many times?" I asked. The coroner had determined Knox's skull had been hit at least six times. Three, he said, were likely administered post-mortem.

Cynthia looked at me, her eyes moist. "I don't know," she said. "I can't remember. Probably three. But I was in such a state, it might have been more. Or less. I just don't recall."

"I see," Davis said. "What did you do next?"

"I turned around and left," she said. "Got in my car and drove back to Boston. I don't remember anything about that trip either. I don't know how I got back. I just remember pulling into Mother's home and stopping in front of the garage there. I sat there for a long time. Then I got out, went inside and just continued my daily activities."

"We interviewed the servants at your mother's house," Jonah said. "They all said that when news of your husband's murder came later in the day —the Belmont Police sent out an officer — you reacted emotionally. A doctor had to be called and a sedative was administered."

"That's probably right," she said. "I must have lost it at that point. It all came crashing down on me."

"Where was Preston standing when you … when you attacked him?" I asked.

"I - I think it was in the dining room," she said. "I don't really recall. Maybe it was in the kitchen. I just don't remember."

Jonah and I looked at each other. Preston's body had been found halfway into the kitchen, with his lower extremities still in the dining room.

"Okay," Davis held up a hand in the stop signal. "Jonah, please take Mrs. Knox and her counsel to Interview Room Two. We will conduct a formal interview there. Mrs. Knox, when we begin again, we will read you your rights. You already appear to be represented by counsel. I suggest you listen to him and do what he says. At the conclusion of that interview, the state of Rhode Island may decide to file charges against you. We will inform you at that time of what actions we will take and what you can expect to happen. Is all of that clear?"

"Yes, Chief," Cynthia said.

"I would like you to sign this waiver of voluntary surrender, please," Davis said. He opened one of his desk drawers and took out a paper. He handed it across his desk along with a pen. Cynthia took the paper and signed it without reading it. Then, she and Elkington stood up and followed Jonah out of the office.

When they were gone, Davis and I looked at each other. I'm sure he had his thoughts about what had just happened. I surely did. But this was not the time nor the place to discuss them.

Instead, Davis picked up his desktop phone and punched in some numbers.

"Mary Jane?" he said when someone answered. "I need the Colonel, right now." There was a pause while Colonel Jefferson Wadsworth's secretary explained what the head of the Rhode Island State Police was doing, hopefully someplace else in the building.

"MJ?" Ruggerio cut her off. "I don't give a rat's ass what the man is doing. I need to talk to him and I need to talk to him right the fuck now!"

I pushed myself off the wall and left Davis' office. He had police business to do, and telling the head of the agency that the late Attorney General's wife had just confessed to murdering him seemed pretty important.

I met Jonah in the hallway. He had just escorted Cynthia and Elkington into the interview room, where they would be filmed and recorded. I imagined someone from the Attorney General's office, and probably the local U.S. Attorney's office would get an emergency call to come sit in. Then, after several hours of questioning, a decision would be made, charges drawn up and a judge found to hold a preliminary hearing, after which Cynthia would be bound over or, more likely, released on bond. It was the beginning of the process where the case is removed from the hands of the investigators, like me, and turned over to the lawyers.

Jonah looked like he had seen a ghost.

"Can you believe this shit?" he said to me.

"Not really," I said.

He did a double take.

"You don't believe her?"

I shook my head. "Not a word," I said. "Her alibi was already established by the staff up in Boston, she got several details of the crime scene wrong and she's left-handed."

"What?" He was taken aback. "What difference does that make?"

I smiled at him. Young detectives always overlook the details.

"She signed that waiver with her left hand," I said. "But the coroner's report showed that the injuries were inflicted by someone striking with the right hand. The angle of the blows was clearly on the left side of Preston's head. He was killed by a righty."

"So she's lying?" Jonah sounded gobsmacked again. "Then why did she confess?"

"Because she knows who the real killer is," I said. "And she's trying to protect him. Or her. It's got to be one of the kids. She's trying to protect her young."

Jonah thought about that for a minute. Then he shook his head and whistled softly to himself. "Mama Grizzly," he said to himself.

"Exactly," I said.

CHAPTER 14

THE NEWS OF Cynthia Knox's confession to the murder of her late husband leaked. It always does. I would have put my money on the state police PR woman, trying to keep some favorite reporter on her side. But it could have been anyone.

Nevertheless, the story exploded the next morning.

KNOX WIFE CONFESSES TO KILLING was the banner across the top of the Providence Journal's front page. Elkington, her lawyer, was quoted as denying the story, but I knew that Cynthia would be arraigned probably today. The TV stations were running the story as well, with file footage from past appearances by the not-so-happy couple.

Davis Ruggerio had contacted all of us on the Task Force to tell us to keep working,

"We're treating this confession as 'questionable,'" he told us. "Might be genuine, but we can't be sure at this point. Keep digging."

So I called Barrington High, spoke to a nice lady in the principal's office, and made an appointment for that afternoon.

That done, I was enjoying my second, or maybe third, cup of coffee for the morning. Then my phone rang. It was Frannie, the school secretary.

"Hey, Frannie," I said, "What's up?"

"It's bad, Julius," she said. "Can you come over?"

"Is it Mattie?"

"Yup."

"On the way," I said.

When I got to the school building, I went right up to the second floor, where the school administration offices were located. The secretary told me that Francine was in the school nurse's office. I went down the hall and walked in.

Frannie was waiting for me in the outer office. She was sitting behind the small metal desk there, arms crossed, face red. She looked at me and I could feel the anger seeping out of her pores. Her dark eyes flashed and her lips were pursed.

"He came in late today," she told me. "A little over an hour ago. I think he walked to school. His teacher took one look and sent him up here. And called me. So I called you."

"How bad is it?" I said.

Frannie nodded towards the inner office, where the nurse took her patients. I took a deep breath, then opened the door and stepped inside.

Mattie was lying on his back on the padded examination table, on top of that crinkly paper they peel down new for every patient. He was fully dressed — jeans and a sweatshirt —and the nurse had swiveled a round work light over his head and positioned the beam on his forehead. She was dabbing at the abrasions along his hair line with gauze. His lip was swollen on the left side and a small trickle of blood oozed from a cut just under his hair.

Mary Callahan, the school nurse, glanced up at me. "Hey, chief," she said. "Frannie said she'd call you in on this. Save me the trouble."

"Yeah," I said. "I'll take care of the paperwork later."

I went over and squeezed Mattie's shoulder.

"You doin' OK, kiddo?" I said.

He nodded.

"Good," I said. "You just keep still and let Nurse Callahan here do her thing. She'll have you all fixed up in nothin' flat."

He nodded again.

"We'll talk a bit when she's done, OK?"

He nodded.

I gave his shoulder another squeeze and went back to the outer office.

"You call his mother?" I asked Frannie.

She nodded. "Said she didn't have a car. Father's gone again on a job. Not due back for four or five days. Said she'd try and get a neighbor to run her over."

"She sound surprised her husband beat the hell out of him?"

Frannie shook her head, compressing her lips. "Not really," she said. "But I didn't press it."

I nodded.

"When you put that animal away, Jules, you'd better make sure it sticks," she said. "Guys like that, give 'em half a chance, they'll come back and finish the job. And do both the mother and the little sister at the same time." She blew out a breath. "Goddam it to hell."

I went back downstairs and stood outside in front of the school. I called Jessica Martin, Gus' second in command at Little Penwick PD.

"Hey chief," she said cheerfully when I got her on the line. "What good cheer do you have today?"

"I need you to work up some arrest papers, Jess," I said. "Subject name is Hector Gonzales. Lives up in those apartments off Maple. He beat up his boy, Mattias Gonzales, age 12, I think. Sent him to school then took off on a trucking job for the next four, five days. Nurse is cleaning the boy up right now."

Jessica's cheerful demeanor changed, immediately.

"Roger, chief," she said. "Charges?"

"Assault and battery on a minor child," I said. "Child abuse, violence. Child endangerment. Once we interview the mother, there may be a few more we can add in."

I could hear her scribbling all this down as I talked.

"Is it bad?"

"Abrasions on scalp and mouth," I said. "I'll talk to Mary Callahan when she's finished with the boy, see if there's anything else she could find."

"Son of a bitch," she said. "You're sure he's not still in the jurisdiction?"

"Pretty sure," I said. "You can call his employer and find out where they think he is. But the wife said he'd be back in four or five days. You need someone to wait at the town line, you let me know."

"Hear you loud and clear, chief," she said. "But you just let us handle this. It's our job. And I can assure you that we are as mad about it as you are."

"I know, Jess, I know," I said. "It's just …"

"Yes," she said, "It is."

I WENT BACK inside the school and upstairs to the nurse's office. She was about finished with Mattie, who now had a bandaged head and was holding some ice to his swollen lip.

"He need to have a doc look at him?" I asked Mary, the nurse.

"That would up to his mother," she said. "I called her, and she said they couldn't afford it, and to just bring him home." She looked at her patient. "I don't think he has a concussion. I got the cut on his head to stop bleeding. The swollen parts will go down with the ice pack."

"Can I give you a lift home, Mattie?" I said.

He nodded and got up and we walked down the stairs. I got him up in the passenger seat of my car and buckled him in. I got behind the wheel, but didn't start the engine.

"You want to talk about it?" I said to him.

He looked straight ahead, out the window, looking at the front of the school building, and shook his head.

"Sometimes helps if you tell someone what happened," I said. "I called over to the police station where I used to work, and they're gonna send someone over to talk to your mom, find out what happened. Was it your Dad who did this?"

Mattie shook his head again. This time, I saw a tear making its way down his cheek.

"I ran into a door," he said. "It was my fault."

I let that sit there for a moment or two.

"Well, hell," I said, "I guess I'm gonna hafta go arrest that door. Just because you're a door doesn't give you the right to go smacking around my friend Mattie."

He kinda chuckled at that. But said nothing.

I started the car and pulled out of the school lot,

"I understand if you don't want to talk about it," I said. "He's your Dad, and Dad's are special. I get that. Still, there are laws that say you can't just punch out your kid, no matter what. And somebody sure knocked you around a little."

I smiled at him.

"I'll take you home, and when your Dad gets home from his job in a few days, we'll talk to him," I said. "Then we can get this all sorted out."

Mattie sat there, silent as the Sphinx, until I drove the half mile or so and pulled up in the driveway of his apartment building. He got out and started to close the door. Then he stopped and leaned in.

"Wasn't my Dad," he said, and closed the door.

I watched him until he got inside the door to his apartment. I wanted to follow him in and talk to his mother. But

Jessica had told me to butt out and let the police handle the matter, and I knew that they would. So I just sat there, looking at the closed white door for a few minutes. Then I backed out and went home.

CHAPTER 15

My appointment at Barrington High was at three, when most of the school day was over. I got there a little early so I could find the main office. The lady at the front desk told me to take a seat and Principal Alessandro would be right with me.

I sat down next to a girl who was sniffling quietly into a tissue. She had long blond hair which hung straight down framing her face. I tried to guess what year she was, but at that age they all look like seventh graders to me.

"You gotta see the big guy?" I whispered to her conspiratorially. She looked over at me and nodded, eyes still wet.

"I'm an ex-cop," I said. "Don't admit to anything. Ask for a lawyer. If they don't have videotape, you're probably in the clear."

That made her smile. A little.

"Jessica Chapman?" The lady at the front desk called out the name. "You're next." The girl next to me sighed and stood up. She glanced at me briefly.

"Good luck," I said with a smile. She smiled back. I watched as she straightened up, threw her shoulders back and marched through the principal's office door.

"You shouldn't encourage them," the desk lady said to me, frowning.

"Time like this, everyone should hear an encouraging word," I said. "Didn't you ever get called into the school principal's office?"

"I most certainly did not," she said, glaring at me over the tops of her bifocal glasses.

It was another fifteen minutes before the door opened and Jessica walked out, followed by a large, round middle-aged man with greasy strands of hair struggling to cover his mostly balding pate. He had a hand resting on her shoulder.

"Please give Jessica a hall pass, Mrs. Foxman," the man said. "I think we won't see a repeat of her behavior, am I right, Miss Chapman?"

"Yessir," the girl said. She cast her eyes quickly my way and gave me a quick smile. Shielding her hand from the principal standing behind her and to the right, she gave me a thumbs up sign. I smiled and nodded at her.

"Go forth and sin no more," Alessandro said and she disappeared into the hallway. He turned and looked at me.

"Chief Haddock," he said, looking down at me. I felt immediately uncomfortable and tried to remember what I had done. Then I remembered I was here to interview *him*. "Please come in."

His office was large and well lighted. His desk took up much of the room, perfectly situated between two long narrow windows that ran almost all the way between floor and ceiling tiles. There were two guest chairs in front of the desk.

On the wall to the right, there were four wooden shelves full of Barrington High swag and trophies. On the narrow section of wall between the two windows behind his desk, Alessandro had hung framed photos of himself with various famous people: I saw one with a former governor and another with a black man that looked a lot like Big Papi, David Ortiz, formerly a slugger with the Red Sox.

He motioned me into a guest chair and walked around and sat in his power chair. His expansive desk was mostly empty, save for his telephone, a Rolodex, a stapler and a framed photo of his family: the rotund wife and the two kids, girl and boy, all smiling into the camera.

"How can I be of assistance?" he said, cocking his head to one side.

"I'm part of the state police task force investigating the death of Preston Knox," I said. "I'd like to get some information about his son, David Knox."

"Wait," Alessandro said, "Didn't you guys get a confession yesterday from the mother? I saw it in the news last night."

"Yes," I said, nodding at him and smiling pleasantly. "Mrs. Knox has confessed to the crime. However, there are still some loose ends we are trying to tie up in the case."

"I see," he said, tenting his fingers over his lap and looking like he didn't understand at all.

"I don't think we need David's official transcript," I said. "But I would be interested in finding out what kind of student he has been."

"Ah," he said, "I see. As it happens, I do have his transcript here. I had Mrs. Foxman pull it when I heard you were coming over." He flipped open a blue folder and leaned forward to study it more closely.

"This says that David is a good student," he said. "Good, but not great. He has mostly as B average in most of his classes. Does quite well in mathematics and the sciences. Not so well with English and history." He looked up at me. "That's inverted from the median. Typically, boys of his age are good in writing and reading and not so good in math and science."

"I see," I said.

"Behaviorally, he has been fine," Alessandro continued. ":One or two lunchroom demerits, but nothing for the last year. Again, that is typical of his age cohort." He stopped again and looked at me. "A cohort is …"

"I know what the word means," I said. "What are his extra curricular activities?"

Alessandro looked down at the transcript again. "He was in the Chess Club his freshman year, but dropped out after that. That club has a reputation for being somewhat nerdy, I'm afraid. Many boys won't go near it, even if they enjoy the game. Do you play chess, Mr. Haddock?"

"Only with bad guys," I said. "What else?"

Alessandro looked at me as if I had farted aloud. But he dropped his eyes back to the transcript and read some more.

"He joined the golf team last year," he said, his finger pointing to the place on the transcript where it said that. You can talk to Coach Jenkins." He looked at me. "Walter Jenkins teaches biology and coaches. Been here at least ten years now."

"I'd like that," I said. "Is there anything else? What about his friends?"

Alessandro sat back in his leather chair and tented his fingers again.

"Ah, well, the answer to that question will not be found in his official transcript, of course," he said.

"Of course," I repeated.

"But I believe that David has found some companions among the other members of his golf team," he said. "You can ask Mr. Jenkins for more details about that."

"I certainly will," I said. "I have been told that a young man named Daniel Kuhn is probably David's best friend. What can you tell me about him?"

The man's fingers were tented again. Tapping this time. He thought for a moment or two, then exhaled rather loudly.

"Mister Kuhn," he said, as if he were describing the super-villain in one of those superhero movies. "That young man is practically the diametric opposite of Mr. Knox. His grades are barely above fail, although I believe his intelligence quotient is one of the highest in the school. He is a constant challenge to authority. He is entirely unafraid to stand out and be different, which makes him an extremely rare bird in this environment. So many of the children here strive for the camouflage of conformity. Mr. Kuhn does not."

He looked pleased with his turn of phrase. I'm sure it sounded like a good book title to him. The Camouflage of Conformity. A book he would almost certainly never write.

"How does Davie Knox fit into Danny's unconventional world?"

"An excellent question, Mr. Haddock," Alessandro said. "You have heard the saying that opposites attract?"

"I remember that in physics," I said.

He smiled as if I were an idiot.

"I think David likes Danny because of his non-conformity," he said. "Being the son of an important figure like the Attorney General, I'm sure David is under strong pressure to conform, fit in, and achieve. Danny gives him the opportunity to cut loose a little. Let his freak flag unfurl as it were."

I thought about that for a moment. Alessandro sat there looking pleased with himself.

"You seem to have spent some time thinking about all this," I said.

He nodded, trying to look humble.

"Yes," he said. "Part of my job is analyzing these childrens behavioral and psychological inter-relationships. I was two semesters short of attaining my PhD in behavioral psychology. It has been a lifelong area of interest for me."

"I see," I said. "What can you tell me about the relationship between David Knox and his late father?"

"Ah," Alessandro said, eyes lighting up with interest. "That is the crux of the matter, is it not?"

"Crux," I said, nodding.

"Indeed," he said. "I made it a point to get to know Preston Knox, beginning when David's sister Samantha arrived here six years ago. I wanted to nurture that relationship, let the Attorney General know that we valued his participation in our campus life and activities. I felt that would be beneficial both to the Knox children and the greater school community."

"How'd that work out?"

He smiled. "Preston Knox delivered the commencement address at his daughter's graduation," he said. "It was well received by the community."

"I've heard that Knox was always a little disconnected from his children's activities," I said. "Has that been your experience?"

He looked a little troubled. "Not at all," he said. "He has always been welcome here."

"But did he ever come? Like to his kids' events and games and such? Parent-teacher conferences, stuff like that. Did he ever show up?"

Alessandro looked troubled again. "I—I am not sure," he said. "That kind of thing doesn't usually show up in one's transcripts."

"Too bad," I said, standing up. "It's the most important part. Thanks for your time. How can I find Coach Jenkins?"

THE SCIENCE CLASSROOMS were off in their own wing of the school. Probably a safety measure in case the young chemistry students mixed the wrong things together or something. There were long laboratory classrooms so the biology students could slice up frogs, the chemistry students could try to blow things up and the physics brainiacs could get a head start on inventing the process for nuclear fusion.

I walked into the empty lab labeled Biology and saw a middle aged man wiping down a white board at one end of the classroom. He was dressed in chinos, a white oxford shirt and a black tie whose knot rested several inches away from his Adam's apple.

"Coach Jenkins?" I said, to get his attention.

He jumped a little and turned around to look at me. I noticed he had a pack of cigarettes —Marlboros — in his other hand.

"Yes?"

I introduced myself and told him what I was doing there. He listened, nodding.

"Can I ask you a favor?" he said.

"Sure."

"Can we take this out to the faculty parking lot?" he said. "I've been craving a smoke for two hours now, and if I don't have one pretty soon, I may collapse and die."

"Wouldn't want that on my conscience," I said, "Lead on."

He took me down the back stairs and outside. There was a concrete walkway that led to a parking lot tucked away behind the school. Beyond the lot were the athletic fields. On one, the football team was running drills. On another, the girls' soccer team was kicking a white ball around.

Jenkins took me over to a black Honda sedan and opened the front door. He sat down in the driver's seat, fished out a Marlboro, lit it and took a deep inhale that seemed to last for a minute. He held it in for several counts and then let it all out in a massive cloud.

"Thank you sweet Jesus," he said. "I think I'm going to live."

He took another deep drag.

"Unusual to find a biology teacher who's a hard smoker," I said. "Kinda goes against the grain, doesn't it?"

He nodded, unable to speak with his second huge lungful of smoke. He finally let that one out, too.

"Do as I say, not as I do," he said. "The mantra of many teachers."

"Whatever," I said. "What can you tell me about David Knox?"

He looked at me with suspicion. "He in trouble?"

I shrugged. "Don't think so," I said. "We're just crossing all the T's and dotting the I's in this case. Background, y'know?"

He nodded, holding in his third drag. A group of girls walking back towards the playing fields called out. "Hey Mister J!" they said. He kept his head down, but stuck a hand up in the air and waved. He waited a few more seconds until they had passed on before letting out the smoke in another cloudy rush.

"I think they probably all know you're a smoker," I said. "Kids generally pick up on stuff like that."

He nodded and shrugged. "I try not to rub their noses in it," he said. "You never know when one of them will tell their mother and then I'll be in trouble."

"David Knox?"

He smiled and shook his head.

"Kid's a B student," he said. "I had him in class last year. He's a B student in golf, too. Thinks he's just inches away from being one of the all-time greats. But he's not. Hits at the ball, rather than swinging. Needs a lot more upper body strength, but doesn't work at it. Doesn't like to lift weights. Doesn't run, so his lower body strength is crap, too."

He took a final deep drag and dropped his butt on the ground, grinding it into the asphalt with his heel.

"Mentally, he lets the course play him," Jenkins continued. "In competition, he gets anxious, his swing speeds up and then he's all over the map."

"I thought he was your number two player," I said.

Jenkins laughed. "He is," he said. "Benny Tolliver is my one. He shoots 35, 36 for nine on a regular basis. Been playing since he was old enough to walk and has a nice natural swing. He doesn't put a lot of effort into his game, either, which is too bad. He could be good enough to get a college scholarship somewhere if he tried. But most of these kids today don't know what hard work and effort mean."

"So David is just so-so on the course?"

Jenkins nodded.

"I've been told that David and the other guys on the team are pretty close off the course," I said. "True?"

Jenkins shrugged. "Don't really know. I'm their coach, not their best friend. What they do outside school is not my concern."

I stood there for a moment or two, trying to think of anything else I could ask the man.

"I'll tell you one thing about Davy," Jenkins said, closing his car door and preparing to go back inside the school. "He's got a temper on him."

"Really?" I said, "How so?"

He smiled. "Last spring, we had an important match against Portsmouth High," he said. "Position in the state tournament was at stake. David was leading his counterpart by a shot coming down the last. He did a complete choke. Made triple bogey, lost by two. After, he did all the right things—shook hands with his opponent, signed his card. His teammates told him not to worry about it, he'd done his best. But I saw him take his golf bag and walk into the woods near the last hole. He took out every club in his bag and smashed them … every one, against the truck of a tree until they either snapped in two or were bent completely out of shape. Damndest thing I've ever seen, and I've been coaching a long time."

"Wow," I said.

"Yeah," Jenkins said.

CHAPTER 16

It was after lunch the next day that Jessica Martin called me from the Little Penwick PD.

"Hey, Chief," she said. "We picked up Hector Gonzales last night. He got back early. I'm getting ready to interview him."

"Can I come down and listen in?" I asked.

"Sure," she said. "It's your case. Even though you don't actually have cases anymore."

"I don't know what's scarier," I said, "That I understand what you just said or that what you just said made some kind of sense."

She made a noise and hung up.

Half an hour later, I squeezed into the observation room next to the interview room tucked away at the back of the station. There was a one-way glass window/mirror through which I could see Hector Gonzales sitting at the table. His head was down, his hands manacled and fastened to the thick bolt in the top of the table. He looked scared.

Jessica Martin strolled in. She was wearing her commander's uniform: white dress shirt, necktie, blue jacket, blue pants, polished shoes. She had a file folder which she put down on the table and then sat down opposite Hector. He looked up at her.

"Mister Gonzales," Jess began. "Do you know why you're here today?"

"I din do nuffin," he said.

"OK," she said. "Before we begin, I want to read you your rights one more time." She went through the Miranda language in a droney voice. "Do you understand your rights?" she asked when she was finished.

"I din do nuffin," he said.

"We have evidence that your son Mattias was violently attacked a couple days ago," Jessica said. She flipped open her file folder and took out some photos that had been taken at the school nurses' office.

"As you can see in these photographs, taken at the school, Mattias sustained wounds to the top of his head, his eye socket and his mouth. The school nurse recommended sutures, which your wife declined, apparently for economic reasons," Jessica said, laying the photos down on the table, one next to the other. "Did you assault your son, Mister Gonzales?"

He shook his head. "No," he said. "I din do this. I love my boy."

"Why did you leave town immediately after this incident?" Jessica asked.

"I have job," Hector said. "I scheduled to run out to Milwaukee and back."

"That's very convenient," Jessica said. "You assault your son on Tuesday morning and then skedaddle. Let someone else pick up the pieces. Why did you do this? Did Mattie say something that made you angry?"

"I no hit my boy," Hector said again. "I love my kids."

"So who did this?" Jessica waved her hands across the photos showing Mattie's bloody head and face. "If you didn't hit your boy, who did?"

Hector's head fell further down on his chest. "I dunno," he whispered.

"Your wife told our officers that you have been violent with your children in the past," Jessica said next. "She said there have been other incidents when you drew blood or caused bruising on your children. Is that true?"

Hector's head snapped up. "She say that?" he said.

"Yes, she did, Hector," Jessica said.

"Beetch," he said and dropped his head down again.

"OK, Mister Gonzales," Jess said, packing up the photos and returning them to the folder. "Here's what is going to happen next. We are charging you with child abuse and assault and endangerment. You will be taken over to Newport later this afternoon and appear before a judge. He will hold a preliminary hearing on the case and decide if you should be released on bail, or held over until your next court appearance at the Adult Correctional Institute, or the jail. I don't know what the judge will do in your case, but it is likely he will have you put in the ACI to await your trial. Do you have a lawyer?"

Hector was silent. Head down.

"If you do not, the judge will arrange to have one appointed to represent you," Jessica continued. "You should talk with your attorney and do what he or she says. OK, Hector?" Jessica looked at the man, looked into his eyes. "I know this is very stressful and troubling. When you get to the court, you will be able to tell your side of the story. Then the judge will decide what to do. Got it?"

He nodded, and Jessica stood up and walked out of the room. Hector did not move once she had left. He sat there, head down. Jerry Hanlon, one of the patrolmen on the force, came into the room, unclipped Hector from the table, re-clipped his handcuffs behind his back, and led him back to the cells.

I went and found Jessica in her office. She was typing up a report of the interview for the case notes on her computer.

"What do you think?" I asked, as I sat down across from her.

She shrugged and kept typing. "'I din do nuffin,'" she said quietly as she worked. "It's what they all say."

"Yeah," I said, "I suppose. But he didn't strike me as the violent sort."

"He was handcuffed to a table in the middle of a police station," Jessica said, not looking up at me. "What? You wanted him all growling and fighting? That'd convince you he was the perp?"

"You see his reaction when he heard his wife sold him out?" I said.

Jessica shrugged again. "Husbands and wives in abusive homes do not act all Ozzie and Harriet," she said. "I didn't see anything that convinced me he wasn't the one."

She stopped typing on her keyboard and looked at me. "Are you getting soft in your old age?" she said. "I thought you were ready to string this guy up yourself. This one looks so cut and dried you could eat it like jerky. What are you seeing that I'm not?"

I didn't answer at first. I replayed the scene I had just witnessed.

"Were you there when they talked to the wife?" I asked.

She shook her head. "No," she said. "I sent LaToya over with Jerry to talk to her that afternoon. They spent a few minutes with her. Why?"

This time, I shrugged. "Can I talk with LaToya?" I said. "Just like to see what she thought."

Jessica glanced at her watch. "Fine with me," she said. "Sheriff's car should be here in about an hour, take the prisoner over to Newport for his arraignment."

"Thanks," I said, getting up. "Probably nothing."

"I think we can make book on that," Jessica said, and went back to her report.

Back in the squad room, I asked the desk officer, Jerry Hanlon, where LaToya Crenshaw was. He glanced at his watch and nodded toward the front door.

"Four o'clock watch coming in," he said. "She's on the schedule."

Sure enough, by the time I went and poured myself a cup of coffee at the back of the squad room, and stuck my head in the comm room to wave at Dottie, LaToya came in, dressed in civilian clothes and carrying a big bag over one shoulder. Cassie Williams, another of Gus' new hires, came in with her, and the two of them were laughing and talking about something.

They saw me sitting at an empty desk in the squad room and came over to say hello.

"Hey, Chief Haddock," LaToya said with a smile, "Wassup?"

"Not a lot," I said, nodding at Cassie, too. "Have you got two minutes? I want to talk about the Gonzales case."

"Sure thing," she said. "Let me put my stuff in the locker. I'll be right with you."

I nodded and she disappeared. It was about three minutes before she was back. This time, she was dressed in her patrol uniform, gun on her hip, pens tucked in her front shirt pocket, ready for work.

She plopped down at the desk I was sitting at. "Shoot," she said.

"You went to interview the mother," I said. "After they patched Mattie up at the school." She nodded. "Notice anything unusual at home?"

She pursed her lips, thinking. Then she slowly shook her head.

"Not really," she said. "House was a bit of a mess, I remember. Some dishes in the sink and the trash needed taking out."

"Was the girl there?" I asked. "Mattie's sister?"

LaToya nodded. "Yeah," she said. "Attached to her mother's hip the whole time. Sucking her thumb, holding on to her dress for dear life."

"Figures," I said, nodding. "Cops bring your brother home from school with a bandaged head. Might make any kid fearful."

She nodded. "One thing I do remember, seemed at little strange to me," LaToya said.

"What?"

"When we first walked in, Mattie was sitting there, playing with a video game or something. She told Mattie to go to his room," she said.

"OK," I said. "What's strange about that?"

"I don't know," she said. "Maybe it was the tone of her voice. It was cold. She didn't say 'Mattie, babe, would you mind letting me and the police lady talk for a minute?' It was like an order. 'Get in your room.' I thought it a little strange, given what the kid had been through."

"What did he do?"

"Put down his game and went to his room," she said. "No whining, no backtalk. He skedaddled."

"OK," I said. I was struggling to understand. LaToya saw it on my face.

"There wasn't a feeling of mothering, is all I'm saying," she said. "She was pretty cold. And her son had been injured. I guess I was expecting a different reaction."

Jerry Hanlon, manning the front desk, was listening. I looked over   at him across the desks in the bullpen.

"Jerry — you get the same feeling?"

"I thought she was kinda cold, yes," he said. "Not sure if it made the same impression on me as LaToya."

"OK," I said, "What else?"

"We asked if Hector had ever been violent to Mattie before," she said. "She said yes, he has hit the children … both children, many times. She said he believed in discipline for his kids."

"So her testimony is that he has been violent before," I said.

LaToya nodded. "I asked where he was, and she said he had left on a job early that morning. He's a longhaul truck driver for Consolidated. They're up in Seekonk."

"What time did she say he left?"

"I don't remem …" She stopped and pulled her notebook out of her front pocket. She flipped through the pages until she found her notes from the interview.

"Here it is," she said. "She said Mr. Gonzales had left early that morning, before six. His rig had been loaded the night before and was waiting at the trucking company."

"Was Mattie up that early?" I asked.

She looked at her notes, then at me. "Don't know," she said.   "We didn't ask that." She paused, "What are you thinking?"

"Not thinking anything," I said. "Just gathering facts and a timeline. Maybe you should go talk to the school nurse again. Find out how old she thinks the injuries on his head were. If they were crusted over, with bruises and all, then maybe Mattie was up before six so his Daddy could smack him around. But when I was there, his wounds were still fresh, still bleeding. Maybe they happened after Hector left for work."

"Which might mean Hector didn't smack his kid around," LaToya said, nodding. "Maybe it was the Mom."

"Or someone else," I said.

LaToya looked across the room at Jerry Hanlon, sitting at the entrance desk.

"You hear all that, Jer?" she said.

He nodded and glanced at his watch. "We could maybe catch the nurse right now," he said.

"Let's ride, cowboy," LaToya said. They jumped up and started to leave. Jerry stopped and looked at me. "Freddie is supposed to be here to relieve me," he said. "Should be here in a few minutes."

"Go on," I said. "I can cover the front desk until he gets here."

Jerry nodded at me and led the two of them out the door. I got up and took my coffee over to the front desk. I sat down. Moved the big calendar blotter back an inch. Moved the telephone console an inch to the right.

"What the hell are you doing, Dad?"

Gus was standing in the doorway to the squad room.

"Jerry and LaToya had to go interview a witness over at the school," I said. "I told Jerry I'd cover the front desk until Freddie gets in."

"Do you know what the insurance company would do if they found out the station was being operated by non-employees?" he said, voice raised a bit.

"No," I said. "But I'll bet it involves paperwork in triplicate."

Freddie Benes pushed in the door from outside, then came into the squad room. He saw Gus and me staring at each other.

"Sorry," he said to Gus. "Got stuck behind the school bus."

Gus didn't say a thing, but turned on his heel and disappeared into his own office.

Freddie looked at me. "Where's Jerry?" he asked.

LaToya and Jerry were back within 30 minutes. They both looked thoughtful.

"Nurse says the wounds on Mattie were fresh," Jerry said. "Took her about fifteen minutes to get his head wound to stop bleeding. That means he was injured just before he arrived at school."

"Frannie told me it seemed he walked that morning," I said. "The Gonzales' apparently only have one car, and Hector took it to work."

"So Maria clipped the kid and then sent him off to school?" LaToya said, her voice rising in outrage. "I told you she was a cold one. That's brutal."

"If it happened like that," I said. "Maybe we should talk to her again."

"What do you mean we?" my son said as he came back into the bullpen. "Jerry, LaToya … you go back and talk to the Gonzales woman again. Tomorrow morning."

They both nodded and looked at me. I shrugged. What could I do? Not my department. Not my case. Just my little pal.

CHAPTER 17

Jerry Hanlon had worked for me for several years, and he understood me. So he called me the next morning and told me that he and LaToya had set up a meeting with Maria Gonzales for ten o'clock.

"Just in case you happen to find yourself outside the home right about then," he said.

I thanked him for the tip.

Maple Street made a loop up to the north from the town center, and then right over to Easterly Road. But just before it made its turn, there was a side street called Finnegan Way, heading off to the west, maybe a quarter-mile long, ending in a patch of trees. On both sides, there were apartment houses, all identical, two stories high, with four units in each: two in the front, two in the back. Each block of units had wide driveways with lots of parking, and those driveways were usually full of kids tricycles, balls, regular bikes and more.

I remembered, vaguely, when the developer, Mr. Finnegan, came down from Fall River in the mid-1970s and proposed this complex to the town planning board and then the council.

There had been a ton of pushback. The opponents claimed Little Penwick was a single-family kind of town and didn't need apartments. Those tended to draw the wrong kind of people: lower income, blue collar workers who made lots of kids who would likely overrun the public school.

The proponents argued that Little Penwick actually needed lower-cost housing for the town's working class, since there was almost no place else in town that was affordable for this income group. Nobody, in the spirited discussion that followed, used the words "black," "Hispanic," or any other racially charged term, but everyone understood that that's what the argument was all about.

This all happened before I signed on as a young patrolman in the Little Penwick force, after getting back home from Nam. But even though the town council eventually approved Finnegan's plans and the complex was built, people talked about it for ten years more. Nobody likes change. Nobody likes new things. Especially people in small towns, who like to be witch-burners against anyone they deem as different.

The Gonzales family rented one of the ground-floor back apartments, about halfway down Finnegan Way. As a police officer and then as chief, I knew this street as one that frequently had domestic disputes, neighbor-on-neighbor disagreements that occasionally got violent, and a lot of weekend drinking. But despite the unspoken fears of the people back then, most of the tenants of these apartments were white people. Working class white people, to be sure, given all the pick-up trucks that were parked along the street. But the Gonzales family was not the only Hispanic one on the block, and there had recently been two black families that had moved in as well. There had been no riots. Witch burners are mostly all talk, no action.

I was parked in my own SUV outside the Gonzales apartment when the town squad car pulled up. Jerry and LaToya got out and came over to my car.

"Always surprised when I drive down this street," LaToya mused as she looked up and down the street. "It's like this little ghetto right in the middle of Little Penwick."

"You know how much average monthly rent is for these units?" I asked. "About fifteen hundred."

LaToya exhaled loudly. "No shit? That's more than I pay up in Warren," she said. "Pretty expensive for a ghetto."

"What's the plan?" I asked.

"Lieutenant Martin wants us to interview Maria Gonzales, Mattie's mother, and get her side of the story. What she knows. Press her a little on the timing of events."

"And maybe we can get Hector out of jail," I said.

She looked at me sideways. "You defending that guy?" she said, sounding surprised. "I thought you and little Mattie were BFFs."

"Beefs?" I said, sounding confused.

She chuckled. "Best friends forever," she said. "So what gives?"

"I'm not defending him," I said. "I'm gathering factual information. Nobody has yet said they witnessed Hector Gonzales hitting his kid. Didn't you and Jerry survey the neighbors?"

"Yeah," she said, tapping the roof of my car with her gaudily painted fingernails. "All the neighbors said he was a good dad. Took 'em fishing and went to their ball games, when he was home."

"No indications of physical violence? Punching, slapping, yelling?"

She nodded. "Nope."

"So," I said. "Let's go see what the Mom has to say."

"You're coming inside, too?" LaToya said, looking surprised.

"He needs to find out what's going on at the home of his new beef," Jerry said with a smile, looking at LaToya. "And when Chief needs to know something, he goes inside."

She shrugged. "OK by me," she said. "Regulations be damned."

"You let me worry about the regs, probie," Jerry said.

She snapped off a mock salute. I liked this girl. She had spirit.

We walked down the walk to the rear apartment on the ground floor. It was Number 23. LaToya knocked on the door. I stood back a bit, behind the two officers.

The door was opened by a little girl, maybe five years old, who had curly ringlets wreathing her face and cascading down onto her shoulders. She was clutching a stuffed doll in a yellow dress. She looked at us with big brown eyes the size of silver dollars. She didn't say anything, just stood there looking at us.

"Hi, honey," LaToya said. "Your Mom home?'

The girl nodded, then opened the door further, turned and walked into the house. LaToya, Jerry and I followed.

The apartment was laid out in a standard manner. The front door opened into the large living room space. Next to it was the kitchen, separated by a pass-through counter. A hallway ran down to the back, where there were two bedrooms and a bath at the end of the hall. The floor was covered with gold plush carpet that had seen better days. The living room had a threadbare sofa, a large screen TV, two metal folding chairs and a small table in front of the couch. There was an overhead light on the ceiling.

I glanced over at the kitchen. The sink had what looked like a day's worth of dishes stacked down inside. There was a black frying pan on one of the stove burners, with the remnants of what looked like scrambled eggs. There was a ceiling fan in the kitchen, which was lazily spinning around and around, silently.

"Where is your Mommy?" Jerry asked the girl.

"Sleeping," she said, hugging the doll closer.

"Can you go wake her up?" LaToya said. "We need to speak with her for a minute."

The girl nodded, and went down the hall. We waited. We heard the girl say something, and heard an adult voice say "What?" There was a pause. "Who is it?" the adult voice said. Pause. "Aw, shit."

A few moments later, Marta Gonzales came down the hall, rubbing her eyes and tugging at her T-shirt to close the gap of stomach skin that had been visible. The little girl came after her, holding the yellow doll closely next to her face.

"What is this?" Marta said. "What are you doing in my house?"

"Miz Gonzales," LaToya said, stepping forward and taking charge. "We're from the Little Penwick Police Department. I am Officer Crenshaw and this is Officer Hanlon and former chief Haddock. We'd like to ask you a few questions about your son Mattias and what happened to him the other day."

"I already tole them about this," Marta said. "Why do I have to do this again?"

"We just have one or two questions," LaToya said. "It won't take long."

Marta turned to look at the little girl.

"Maria," she said sharply. "Go to your room."

The little girl looked at her mother. Then she looked at us. But she stood there.

"Did you hear me?" Marta said, her voice raised. "Go to your room. Right NOW!"

The girl flinched at her mother's shout. But she turned and disappeared down the hallway. We heard a door close.

Marta turned back to us.

"What questions?" she said.

LaToya took out her notebook and pen and flipped through a few pages.

"On the morning of the incident with Mattias, did you take him to school?" she said.

"No," Marta said. "He ride the bus, like always. Or he walk, ride his bike. Is not far."

"He had a serious head wound," LaToya said. "He was bleeding. Yet you let him walk to school like that?"

"Not bleeding then," Marta said. "He ride bike like always. He fine."

Her eyes darted back and forth between LaToya and me. She was looking to see if we were buying that.

"The trucking company told us that your husband reported for work that morning just after six a.m.," LaToya said. "The school said Mattie arrived that day at a quarter to eight. When did your husband strike Mattias?"

"Before he leave," she said.

"So you found him injured, when?"

"I get up later," Marta said. "Maybe seven, seven-thirty."

"And you saw that his head was injured, that there was bleeding on his skull?"

"Yes."

"And that he had been struck in the eyes, lips and cheek."

"Yes."

"Why didn't you call the police?"

Marta didn't answer. She walked over and sat down on one of the two metal chairs.

"Why you ask me these things?" she said. "My husband did this. He in jail right now. You should go ask him these questions."

"We're asking you, Mrs. Gonzales," LaToya said. Her voice was firm, but not threatening. Good interview technique. I wondered if they had taught that in the academy, or if LaToya was just a natural. I suspected the latter.

"I not know," she said. "I get up from my bed. Maria is crying. Mattias wants his cereal. I look at clock, he has missed the bus. I tell him to ride the bike. I not really notice if anything is wrong."

"You said you saw his head was bleeding and that he had been struck in the face," LaToya said. "But you didn't call anyone for help, but just sent him to school like normal?"

"Yes," she said. She looked at us with her lower lip pursed outwards. Go ahead, challenge me, it seemed to say.

LaToya didn't say anything, but looked at the woman. She was small, perhaps five feet. She had wide hips and her face was beginning to round out like older Mexican women's do. She looked uncomfortable, as if she knew her story was not quite adding up.

Out of the corner of my eye, I saw a little head peek around the doorway to the hall. It was Maria, still clutching her doll. Marta saw her at about the same time. She grabbed a coffee mug that was sitting on the table and hurled it across the room towards the girl.

"I tole you to go to your room!" she screeched. The mug shattered against the wall. Maria disappeared back down the hallway.

LaToya flipped her notebook closed. "OK, Mrs. Gonzales," she said calmly. "That'll be all, for now. Thank you for talking with us. We may have some follow-up questions later, if that's OK with you?"

Marta nodded. "Sure, sure," she said.

We left her sitting there and went back out to their squad car. Jerry got in behind the wheel.

"What do you think?" I asked.

"Gonna call Children and Family Services," she said. "Get an abuse counselor down here stat. That woman is nuts."

"Still think Hector hit the kid?"

She paused, thinking. "Looks more doubtful," she said. "But I'm gonna get the professionals in here first. Then we can make up our minds."

I nodded. "Good plan," I said.

CHAPTER 18

Tʜᴀᴛ ɴɪɢʜᴛ, I prepared dinner for Siggi. She'd apparently been busy at the doctor's office and with her grown daughters, since I hadn't seen her for a couple of days. Three, in fact. Not unusual in our lives, but a little out of the ordinary.

She came in, hung up her coat and gave me a big hug.

"Missed you, babe," I said, my face tucked into her fragrant hair.

"No you haven't," she said, pulling back but looking up at me with a smile. "You've been involved in your case. And that means you haven't been thinking about anything else."

I thought about that. "Yeah, I guess you're right," I said. "So what have you been up to the last three days?"

She rummaged around in the fridge and pulled out a half-full bottle of wine. She uncorked it, smelled it to make sure it hadn't turned, and poured herself a glass. She motioned to me to ask if I wanted a glass, too, but I nodded at my beer, that had been helping me make dinner.

"Well," she said, "In addition to work and helping my daughter, I've been doing a little investigation of my own."

"About what?"

"Deke Scanlon," she said, her eyes glistening with excitement. "And his secret past."

"Really?" I said. "Well, let me get dinner on the table and you can tell me the whole thing."

I had roasted some chicken breasts slathered with apricot jam, made a pot of Moroccan couscous and tossed a green salad. The table was already set, so I filled up two plates, set them on the table and got a new beer for me out of the fridge. Siggi put a couple of candles in the middle of the table, lit them and we sat down and clinked glasses.

"So," I said, after we had eaten for a while. "Tell me what you've learned about our town grump."

"It took me a couple of days," she said, color alight in her cheeks. "I started in the library and then moved over to the Little Penwick Historical Society. You know Agnes Collins, right?"

I nodded. Agnes was a woman in her eighties who knew more about the history of our town, and the families that created it, than anyone else I knew. The Historical Society owned an early eighteenth century house and an acre or two of what had been the Gilcrest Farm, and gave tours and talks in the summer months. The old farmhouse was now a museum of sorts, with lots of photos and artifacts from the time when Little Penwick, like most old towns in New England, had been an agricultural town, except for the fishermen who lived down around the harbor.

"Well, she told me the history of the Scanlon House," Siggi said. "It was built up there on the Long Highway, just across from Scanlon Pond and near the old grist and lumber mills, sometime around 1790. Several generations of Scanlons lived there over the decades."

"They tore it down sometime in the Fifties, I think," I said. "I guess it got too old to keep up anymore."

"That's what they told the rest of the town," Siggi said, her eyes excited again. "But Agnes told me the real story was quite different. And it involved Deke, the younger son of Frank Scanlon, Junior who was the fifteenth direct descendant of Abraham Scanlon, the man who dammed up the pond and built the mills."

"Are you going to list all the descendants?" I said. "Cause if you are, I might need a whiskey chaser for my beer."

"I have them all written down, in order, with wives and offspring," Siggi said, "But I'll spare you the details."

I raised my beer glass in a mock toast.

"So Frank Scanlon, Junior was born in 1901," she said. "He married one of the Jeffords girls and they had two sons. Frank the Third, or Trippy, was the oldest and Deke was a couple years behind him. Agnes Collins told me that the two boys were inseparable as children, but also very competitive, being just two years apart in age."

"Uh-oh," I said, "I smell a family problem coming."

"Oh, yes," Siggi said, drinking some of her wine. "It was probably inevitable. Frank Junior, the boys' father, was old-school. Probably all the Scanlons before him had been, too. When the boys came back from the war — Trippy had been with the Marines in the Pacific while Deke was in the Navy, running cargo and equipment across to England — Frank sat them down and told them that Trippy, as the eldest son, was going to inherit the bulk of the Scanlon estate: the lumber mill, the pond and the old mansion. Deke was going to get a few acres north of the pond, a little money and not much else."

"If I were Trippy, I'd be watching my six," I said. "Nothing worse than a pissed-off sibling."

"At first, everything was fine," Siggi continued. "Frank the Third married one of the Goulds over in Newport. She had a ton of family money of her own. They had about six kids. Took over the mansion."

"And Deke?"

Siggi frowned. "He went out West. Did some ranching in Montana, then some wine-making in Napa."

"Trying to make his own way in the world," I said. "Good for him."

"But in the mid 1950s, Deke came back to Little Penwick," Siggi continued. "Nobody is quite sure why. He never said. But that's when the trouble started."

"He wanted his share," I said.

Siggi shook her head, "No," she said, "It was a woman."

I thought about that. Almost said, out loud, *it's always a woman, isn't it*? But I didn't.

"Picture this," Siggi said. "Deke is home after ten years away. Trippy throws a party to welcome him back. Now this is in that big old Scanlon manion. Frank Junior is still alive, but their mother has passed. With the six kids and the rich mother who probably couldn't be bothered with actual child-rearing, they had servants. Lots of them. Mostly import-ed from Ireland."

"Young lassies from the Old Country," I said. "I think I see where this is going."

"Yes," Siggi said. "At the party, Deke couldn't take his eyes off one of the servers. Her name was Siobhan O'Malley. She came from Galway. She was maybe twenty years old. Deke was now around thirty-five."

"And Old Eros shot them both full of lead," I said.

Siggi smiled at me. "I think he used arrows, but yes. They both fell immediately and deeply in love."

"Wait," I said, holding up a hand. "I thought Deke Scan-lon was a lifelong bachelor. I've never heard of any Mrs. Scan-lon, Siobhan or anyone else."

"And now you're going to hear the rest of the story," Siggi said. "Agnes Collins told me what she had heard and I con-firmed it in the town records kept at the library."

I sat back. "This is good," I said. "Continue."

"So Deke goes to see his father, tells him he's in love with one of the Irish servants and they intend to marry as soon as possible," she said. "Frank Junior — who is old-school, re-member — flies off the handle and forbids the marriage. Dis-inherits the man and, just to make sure he will never inherit anything of value, Frank decides to tear down the old house."

"What did Trippy think of that idea?"

Siggi smiled. "Trippy's wife was from the Gould family over in Newport," she said. "Her great-great was Jay Gould who helped build the railroads and then became one of the country's richest men. One of those robber baron types from the Gilded Age. She came from wealth and still had plenty of it. So they bought a little mansion on Ocean Drive and moved the kids over there. Frank Junior pulled down the ancestral home."

"What did Deke do?"

"There was not much he could do," Siggi said. "He married Siobhan anyway, in 1954. Two years later, she was dead. I think they said it was from a bad case of influenza, but Agnes said the town gossips all believed she died of a broken heart, because she felt she had come between her man and his family."

"Wow," I said. "That's an incredibly sad story. In so many ways."

"But there is a point to it, that concerns the Deke of today and his land above the pond," Siggi said. "Guess where Siobhan Scanlon is buried?"

"Not in the town cemetery, I'm guessing," I said.

She shook her head. "She was interred in a private grave somewhere on the land that Deke Scanlon owns near the pond. Near his cottage out there. Nobody in the town is really certain of the exact location. They told me they had long since lost the records of the place of burial. 'It's up in those woods somewhere' they told me. At that time, apparently, back in the Fifties, it was still possible to arrange for private burial on your own land."

I thought about that.

"So that's why he doesn't want to sell the land," I said. "He wants to protect his wife's burial plot."

"I think that is right, yes," Siggi said. He very likely intends to be buried next to her some day. And he knows that any new owner of that land, especially any kind of developer, will likely petition the town to have the graves moved, back to the town cemetery."

I was nodding. "I'll talk to Billy Church," I said. "I'll bet the Land Trust can put some kind of codicil into the transfer agreement that says they'll leave the grave sites untouched and maintained for eternity. Once the story gets out, it may attract romantic pilgrims, to see the place where the ill-treated lovers are buried."

Siggi shook her head and frowned. "I don't think Deke would be interested in becoming a romantic hero," she said. "I think he'd rather be left alone."

What she said made a lot of sense. But I would talk to Billy and then arrange to go see Deke again. We might be able to work something out.

I raised my beer bottle again. "That was some excellent detective work," I told Siggi. "If you ever decide to stop nursing the kiddies, there'll always be a job for you at Julius Haddock Investigations."

Siggi laughed. I always loved hearing that laugh.

"You and I could never work together," she said, eyes bright. "We'd kill each other inside of a week. Our House of Work signs are complete opposites. Sharp angles."

"Wouldn't that work better?" I said. "You do the things I hate to do, and vice versa?"

"No," she said, shaking her head. "It would be much better if we didn't work together, except on these little things that we can do apart. Trust me on this."

I did trust her. So I dropped it. For now.

CHAPTER 19

The task force assembled again the next morning. It was raining, hard, and the traffic coming into town was ridiculous. Whenever it rains in Rhode Island, which is frequently, the citizens of the state automatically forget how to operate a motor vehicle.

So I just barely made it to the conference room in time. And I didn't have a chance to get myself some coffee before the meeting began. That and the idiots I had been dodging on the highway made me a little edgy.

"OK," Davis said, calling us to attention. The room settled down. "Let's get started. Jonah…anything new?"

"Yeah, chief," he said. "We just got the call records from the phone of Camilla DeRosa, one of the girls Preston Knox was allegedly bumping during the campaign."

The room began tittering again. Davis held up a hand and it stopped.

"I've looked at her calls on the day of Preston's murder," he said. "She called his private cellphone at seven-fifteen a.m. Call lasted twelve minutes. My people are going through the records right now, looking for other times and dates when the two of them talked."

"Seven fifteen would have been around the time David Knox came downstairs for breakfast," I said.

"You're back on the kid again," Jonah said, rolling his eyes in my direction. "You're not giving up on him, are you?"

"Last one to see Knox alive," I said. "Until proven innocent, he's still a prime suspect in my book."

"Time for a new book, old man," Jonah said. There were twitters in the room again.

Ruggerio looked up and the room went silent.

"Let's bring this DeRosa woman in and find out what she was talking about with the Attorney General at seven in the morning," he said. "Then we can decide if we need to talk to David Knox again."

He looked around the room.

"Anything else?" No one spoke. "Okay," he said, "Back to work."

I followed Davis back down the hall to his office. I noticed that Jonah Allen stayed in the conference room to chat with some of the other members of the task force. Probably talking about that crazy old man from the boonies the governor had appointed to the task force who didn't know his ass from his elbow. The young whippersnappers are like that.

Davis heaved himself into the chair behind his desk with a sigh. There were dark circles under his eyes.

"You OK, Davis?" I asked.

He looked at me and shook his head.

"Got a call last night from the governor," he said. "She wanted a progress report."

"OK," I said. "That's normal, right?"

"No," he said. "I don't get calls from the governor. That's Wadsworth's job. I'm just a cop."

"What did she say?"

"Wanted to know if we were going to charge Cynthia Knox," he said.

The assistant attorney general of Rhode Island, Wendella Simpson, who had been one of Knox's harem and was now acting AG for the state, had taken Cynthia Knox's confession under advisement. That meant she was looking at it closely and was going to decide if and when to press charges. It had been several days, so I suspected the AG's office had as many questions about the confession, and its authenticity, as most of us did. The FBI had re-interviewed Cynthia's mother and her household staff, and none of them said Cynthia had been absent that morning. Certainly not for the three or four hours it would have taken her to drive to Barrington, knock her husband in the head, and drive back to Cambridge. To believe that would be a stretch, a huge stretch.

"What did you tell her?"

Davis shrugged. "Told her the AG had the case and was going to decide how to proceed," he said.

"She buy that?"

"Not much she can do," Davis said. "AG looks at the evidence we present and makes the decision to pull the trigger or toss it back. Governor wants the case resolved before the election in two weeks."

"Meanwhile, your head is in the vise," I said.

"And gets tighter every day," he said, with a wry smile.

"Must be why they pay you the big bucks," I said.

He looked at me and laughed. Showed his teeth and everything. I joined in with his laughter. Not much else we could do. Political interference, public pressure … these were all common elements of a major investigation. You either dealt with it, or you found some other line of work. I've heard managing a Christian Science reading room is mostly stress-free.

Jonah Allen bounced into Davis' office.

"Preston and his co-ed talked twenty-three times in the three weeks before his murder," he announced. "He really was a hound, wasn't he?"

"What the hell does a girl like that get from having an affair with someone like Preston Knox?" Davis Ruggerio said. "I mean, I understand what he gets from the deal …"

"His rocks off," Jonah said with a smirk.

"But what could she possibly be hoping for?" he continued.

"Maybe a job in the governor's office," I suggested. "A chance at power and influence? Make her feel more important than anyone else she knows at school, even the professors. Or maybe something even simpler."

"Get her rocks off," Jonah said.

We all chuckled.

"I don't know," Davis said. "We'll probably never know. I just think of my two daughters, both of them happily married and one with a family. I just can't picture either one of them doing something like that."

"If they did, Davis," I said, "They'd probably rather die that have you know about it."

"Because they know I'd kill them if I found out," he said. He was a large man, with a square jaw and big meaty hands. You wouldn't want someone like him to be angry with you.

"Has anyone learned where Judge Cabot was that morning?" I asked. "That's still a loose end."

Davis held up his hand and smiled behind it.

"I called someone I know at the U.S. Marshall's office up at the federal courthouse in Boston," he said. "Used to work for me for years before he moved up there. He told me it's fairly common knowledge among the agents up there that Judge Cabot has a little something going on the side. Likes to meet up with her couple mornings a week."

"This is the guy who thought Knox wasn't good enough for his sister?" I said.

"You're just learning that most people are rank hypocrites?" Davis said. "The good judge forgets that the Marshall service has to keep close tabs on all the judges. How they keep them safe. So whether he knows it or not, they follow him everywhere he goes."

"Geez," Jonah said. "What a family."

I thought of Tolstoy's line again, but let it pass. The philosophy of a 19th century Russian writer didn't exactly fit in a 21st century murder investigation, no matter how apt.

"When is the co-ed coming in?" Davis asked.

"Sarah is on her way right now to pick her up," Jonah said. "Should be back here in an hour. Maybe less."

"Okay," Davis said. "Put her in Room 2 and let her stew for a few minutes."

I stood up and glanced at my watch. "I'll be back in an hour," I said. "Got someone to see."

It took me ten minutes to drive over to Olneyville, one of Providence's more sadsack neighborhoods. But that was where Maggie Wells, my son Gus' intended and soon to be baby momma, ran her counseling center for battered women. I parked on the street outside, hoping no one would key the side of the car or snap off a mirror, just for fun, and went inside the Sunrise Center, nodded at the old guy who served as the center's security man, and knocked on the open door of Maggie's office.

"Julius!" she said, looking up from a raft of paper on her desk. "What brings you to town?"

"State police gave me an hour before we start applying the thumb screws to some poor schmuck of a witness," I said. "So I thought I'd drop in, see if you wanted a cup of coffee or anything."

Maggie, who was six months pregnant, and looked every day of it, looked down at her desk, looked up at me and grinned.

"Oh, hell yes!" she said. "The stuff the state makes us keep track of … drives me nuts! I could use a break."

We went back out to the sidewalk, and Maggie pointed to a hole-in-the-wall diner just across the street and down a ways. The sign above the door said it was the Rainbow Room.

"Is this the Olneyville branch of the one in Rockefeller Center?" I asked.

Maggie smiled. "This place is owned by a couple gay guys from East Providence," she said. "Which probably makes them immune from copyright suits."

Inside, there were a smattering of tables in front of the windows looking out at the street, a wooden bar that had seen better days, and behind the bar some fancy looking espresso machines, all brass piping and glass containers. The wall behind was painted in that symbolic rainbow.

I ordered a couple of cappuccinos and we took a seat at one of the round tables.

"How you feeling these days?" I asked while we waited for the fancy machines to whirr and whoosh and steam.

"Awful," she said. "Back aches constantly, my nipples are sore to the touch and you don't wanna hear about the hemorrhoids."

"I think I just did," I said. "Thanks for that. But I'm sorry for all the aches and pains."

She wiggled around a little on her small metal chair, trying to find a comfortable position and then laughed. She reached her hand out and touched my arm.

"I'm sorry, Jules," she said. "That was just unloading. You didn't do anything to cause my discomfort, except maybe for making Gus in the first place. I blame all of this on him."

Our coffee arrived, along with a plate of those round, stick-like Italian cookie things. Maggie grabbed one and made it disappear.

"You gotta eat the rest," she said, her mouth full of crumbs. "I've been eating like a pig. My OB says I've gained enough weight already and I still have almost three months to go."

"How's the house coming?"

Gus had found a couple acres overlooking a pond in Little Penwick and was building a new home for Maggie and the baby. A good thing, since he had been renting a garage apartment while Maggie still had a loft in one of the old mill conversions in Providence.

"It'll be a race," she said, sipping some coffee. "Which will be here first … the house or the baby. Gus promised the house will be ready by Christmas, but I'm a little doubtful."

"If he says it'll be done, you can probably take that to the bank," I said. "He's always been good at getting things done in time. I think the Army trained him well."

"Yeah, you're probably right," she said. "I'm the skeptic in the family."

"Good to have one of those," I said. "Keeps everyone honest."

We sat there drinking coffee for a minute or two. There were a few other people in the place, and others walking by on the street outside.

"You guys close to solving the case on Preston?" Maggie asked. She had worked for Preston Knox. Knew a lot about his past. Which was why she was now running the Sunrise Center.

I shrugged. "Closer than maybe a day or two ago," I said. "You got any insights on little Davie Knox?"

Her eyes widened a bit.

"You liking him for this?" she said. "Wow. That'd be Oedipal."

"He's a definite maybe," I said, "Which is about all we have right now. But he was the last one to see his father alive. And I haven't been able to cross him off the list."

"Well, there were a lot of cross currents in that family," Maggie said. "Preston, I think, liked his daughter more. They were thick as thieves."

"Samantha was studying law at Penn," I said. "Supposedly following in Dad's footsteps."

Maggie nodded. "Yeah, I can see that," she said. "And David was always closer to his mother. He stood next to her in public. Seemed protective and defensive."

She stopped and held her coffee cup thoughtfully.

"Geez, are Gus and I going to be taking sides, see which one is closest to the little bump here?" She patted her belly. "That just seems off, somehow."

"Your parents never had favorites?" I asked.

She shook her head.

"Not that I could tell," she said. "They spent time with all three of us. Mom was good with Mom things, and Dad was good in his own way. But I couldn't begin to guess if either one of them liked one of us more than the others."

I nodded. "That's the way it's supposed to be," I said. "I never experienced any of that, since my Dad died when I was still small. My sister and I got Mom all the time after that. But she called in my uncle Charlie when I was a teenager. He got me into sports, hunting, fishing and all that. So I guess it worked out OK."

"Speaking of Davie, I do remember a Christmas party at the AG's office, a couple of years ago," she said. "I was standing there with some of the other women in the office, and we watched as Preston was talking with some legislative committee chickie-poo across the room. I mean, it was Christmas, everyone was hitting the punch and people were loosy-goosy like Christmas parties can be."

I nodded. "Been there," I said.

"So we all watched when David approached his father and this woman and got in her face. Said 'Don't you have a family to go home to? Why don't you leave mine alone.' Or something like that. He was loud enough that we could hear it across the room."

"Huh," I said.

"Yeah, that's what we all thought," Maggie said. "I mean, it was true that Preston was flirting with the girl. That was his modus operandi. I doubt they were like exchanging numbers or arranging a rendezvous or anything. But the kid was upset, got right up in her grill."

She paused, thinking.

"In a way, I felt kinda sorry for him," she said. "He must have seen this same scene before with his Dad. Many times. No kid should have to go through that."

I glanced at my watch. I needed to get back to HQ. Maggie saw that and struggled to heave herself out of her chair and back onto her feet.

"Thanks so much for the break, Julius," she said, holding onto my arm and reaching up to kiss my cheek. "I needed it. Hope you get the bad guy."

CHAPTER 20

Camilla DeRosa, who, according to the interview report that was in the investigation book had been something of an uncooperative witness when she had been interviewed at Providence College a week or so earlier, came into the state police headquarters breathing fire.

They put her in one of the drab green-painted interview rooms and I watched from the observation room behind the glass mirror when Davis Ruggerio and Jonah Allen went in to do the follow-up interview.

She didn't look the part of a shrinking violet. Camilla was a large girl. Not fat, exactly, but big-boned and strong looking. I could see her as an athlete: maybe a tennis player or a fullback on the soccer field. She was wearing a navy hoodie sweatshirt with 'Friars' across the front, and a pair of jeans. She had a big leather satchel-like bag that she had plumped on the metal table beside her.

Davis and Jonah opened the door and walked in and Camilla didn't even let them sit down.

"What in the ever-loving hell is going on?" she said, her face reddening. She had been holding back her anger for the last hour or so, as the state troopers brought her down to HQ and it now came flooding out in a rush.

"What kind of country is this when the police can come into a classroom and haul me off without a warrant, or a court order, or anything?" she continued her outraged speech. "I demand to speak to the head guy, the commandant or whatever he's called. I'm assuming it's a man, because in this patriarchal society we live in, it's always a man, isn't it? I cannot believe I'm here. Whatever it is, this better be good. My cousin is an attorney, and I can guarantee you that I'll be talking to him before the day is out and there will be a huge lawsuit coming your way."

She seemed to run out of gas toward the end. Davis and Jonah just let her ramble on. When she finally piped down, Davis spoke.

"Miz DeRosa," he said, "I am Davis Ruggerio, head of the Major Crimes bureau of the Rhode Island State Police. This is my assistant, Detective Jonah Allen. We brought you in here today for further questioning in the matter of the recent death of Attorney General Preston Knox."

"I told that woman, that trooper, before that I didn't have anything to do with that," she was getting riled up again. "How many times do I have to tell you that? Do you speak English here?"

"Miz DeRosa," Jonah Allen jumped in. "We have obtained your telephone records, and on the morning Mr. Knox was murdered, there is a record of a call you placed to his private cellphone. How, please, did you obtain Mr. Knox's private number?"

"He gave it to me, of course," she snapped. "Duh."

"For what reason?" Jonah asked.

Camilla glanced furiously back and forth at Davis and Jonah, who sat still and impassive across the table.

"You know the reason," she said. "I told that to the lady officer, too."

"You told Trooper Wilcox that you had been having a sexual affair with Mr. Knox during the time you were working on his election campaign," Jonah said in a flat voice. "Is that true?"

Camilla sat back. "Is that was this is about?" she said, her voice incredulous. "You got your panties all wadded up because Preston and I were a thing? Geez. You guys ever thought about getting a life?"

"Did you call Mr. Knox on the morning he was murdered?" Davis didn't raise his voice, but his question sliced through the room like an axe.

"Okay," she said, sounding a little less sure of herself. "Yeah, I did. Early that morning."

"Seven-fifteen sound about right to you?" Davis said. He held up a print-out that was probably her call list from that day.

"Whatever," she said, waving her hand.

"What was the purpose of the call?" Jonah continued.

She smiled, a thin derisive smile. "To say good morning, Mister Governor," she said.

"And after you greeted him, what did you talk about?"

Camilla began drumming her finger tips on the table. She was getting nervous.

"I asked him how the campaign was going," she said. "We might have talked about some of the other interns on the campaign. I knew most of them pretty well. Press and I liked to gossip a little about them. It was kind of our little private game we liked to play."

"Sounds like fun," Jonah said in a tone that implied the opposite. "Did you and Mr. Knox make any plans to get together again in this phone call?"

She smiled, this time a Cheshire-cat kind of smile that said *I know something you don't.*

"Maybe," she said.

"Maybe?"

"Okay," she said. "Press was all hot to trot. We hadn't seen each other for about ten days. I had a paper to write and then the hockey team was beginning training. I'm starting left defense." She looked at the two cops as if she expected them to break into applause, They didn't. In my little airless observation room, I mentally patted myself on the back. Hockey team. I thought she looked like an athlete.

"When you say Mr. Knox was, and I quote 'hot to trot,' what exactly do you mean?" Jonah said.

Camilla looked at him with pity in her eyes.

"You want the blow-by-blow, don't you?" she sneered. "All the dirty words, the sighs, the suggestive stuff. Gets you off, does it? Perv."

"So you are saying that you and Mr. Knox engaged in what could be called sex talk, is that right?" Davis said.

"Well, he did," she said. "I don't think I was moaning and groaning. He was on about how he needed to see me. Wanting to kiss and lick me here and there. I just played along."

"How long did this sex talk part of the conversation last?" Jonah said.

"I don't know," she said, throwing her hands up in exasperation. "I didn't have a stopwatch. It was just a phone call."

"And how did this conversation end?" Davis said. "Did you arrange a meeting? Set a date and a time?"

"   Naw," she said. "He cut it off. Said he had to go. Don't think he even said bye, tell you the truth."

"So he was just playing? Stringing you along?"

Her face fell a bit. Her eyes went down to the table and then back up at the two men she was talking with.

"I dunno," she said, her voice falling to a whisper. "I thought I overheard someone in the background, someone walking into the room where he was. Then he just said, 'gotta go,' and he hung up."

"Any idea who it was?" Davis asked.

She shook her head. "Nope," she said. "He was at home, so I figured it was someone in his family or maybe his body man who walked in. That guy Jack. He didn't like me."

Jonah made a note in his notebook. Davis stared across the table at the girl. I knew he was thinking about his own two daughters and making mental comparisons between them and the creature sitting across from him.

"Okay Miz DeRosa," Davis said finally. "Thank you for coming in. We'll have someone drive you back to campus. This is a murder investigation, so please don't discuss the details of this interview with anyone. If we need to speak with you further, we will be in touch."

"That's it?" she said, sounding amazed. "Nothing else? No lectures about morality? About sleeping with happily married men?" She paused. "He wasn't, by the way. Happily married I mean. But that's it, really? No parting words?"

Davis stood up and picked up the file folder he had brought in with him.

"Miz DeRosa," he said, "Neither I nor the State of Rhode Island gives a crap about your sex life. Have a good day."

And he turned and walked out.

WE REGROUPED IN Davis' office. I walked in with Trooper Sarah Wilcox. Jonah Allen was already there.

"Well," I said, "She seemed nice."

Davis kept his stone face in place. I think they teach that in State Police Bigshot Academy.

"Let's get David Knox back in," he said. "Schedule it for the morning. I'm sure Councilor Elkington will want to be included."

"Right, boss," Jonah said. He glanced at me, but I tried on my own impassive stone face. I wasn't about to go all *nyah-nyah*, told you so on him. That would be unprofessional. So I kept my nyah-nyahs to myself.

Davis looked at me.

"You got a working theory how it all went down?" he asked.

I shrugged. "Sounds to me like the kid came downstairs, heard his father making love talk to his mistress and lost his nut," I said. "That gives him motive, opportunity and access to the murder weapon. Seems cut and dried to me."

"Well, let's wait and see what the boy has to say for himself tomorrow," Davis said. "Jonah, see if you can get them in here at eleven."

"Right, chief," Jonah said.

"I'll call the governor," Davis said, reaching for the handset.

"And Wadsworth?" I said.

He didn't respond. He just kept punching the numbers into his phone.

AN HOUR LATER, I wheeled into the parking lot of the Little Penwick police station. I went inside and knocked on the office door of Jessica Martin, Gus' second in command. She waved me in.

"What's the latest with the kid, Mattie?" I asked.

She nodded and dug out some files from under one of the three or four stacks on her desk. She opened one and scanned it quickly.

"We filed a notice to drop charges against Hector Gonzales," she said. "Judge approved the motion in light of the report from the Department of Children and Family Services. They did a complete forensic interview of the household and the mother. We have re-filed charges against Marta Gonzales for child endangerment and abuse. She was taken into custody yesterday."

"What happened to the kids?"

"Ms. Gonzales' father, Pedro Simms, asked the court to appoint him as temporary guardian," Jessica told me. "Mattie and his sister will stay with grandpa until CFS can interview Hector and determine his suitability to continue as a parent."

I nodded. I had supervised several child custody cases over the years, and until the state people were satisfied about the parents, the kids were kept apart. They had their own standards and rules, and they would keep after it until they had figured out how to keep the kids safe.

"Is the mother going to get some help?" I asked.

Jessica nodded. "Judge directed she be taken to a hospital for a mental evaluation," she said. "Better place for her right now than jail."

I nodded at that. "Hope she gets some help," I said.

Lt. Martin flipped through the final pages in the file.

"Oh, yeah, Chief" she said. "One more thing. Mattie wanted to get a message to you."

"Me?" I said.

"You," she said. "He wanted to tell you thanks for helping."

I nodded. I put on my impassive stone face. It wouldn't do to have the members of my former department watch as their ex-chief teared up. Wouldn't do at all.

CHAPTER 21

The next morning, Davis Ruggerio was dressed in the full Mounty—the boots, the leather cross sash, the Stetson hat. Jonah wore a business suit. Even I had put on a dress shirt and tie. It was all sort of the equivalent of the black cap that British judges used to don when they had to hand down a sentence of death. We were dressing up to mark the seriousness of the occasion.

Davis reserved the larger of the interview rooms. There were two chairs on the suspect's side of the metal table, and he had brought in three chairs on the other. The lawyer Elkington was pacing outside in the hall, looking sharp as always in his thousand-dollar suit. I wondered if he ever dressed in jeans and an old T-shirt.

The elevator doors opened at the end of the hall and Cynthia Knox came out with her son David. This time, she had dressed him up, too. He wore a blue blazer, white shirt, grey slacks and a rep tie. He looked ill at ease in his fancy clothes. Or maybe it was the occasion that made him seem a bit nervous.

Davis came out of his office, trailed by Jonah.

"Let's go in here," Davis said, opening the door to the interview room. "Miz Knox, I'm going to ask you to wait in the reception area until after the interview."

"This is my son," she said, protesting. "Surely you will let me be with him."

Davis shook his head. Charlie Elkington took Cynthia's elbow and guided her down the hall.

"It's okay, Cynthia," he said. "I will be in the room the entire time and will look out for the boy. You wait down here until we're done."

When Elkington came back, he led David Knox into the room, and the three of us followed. Once we were all seated, Davis reminded everyone that the interview was being filmed and recorded, and listed the names of all of us in the room for the record.

"Good morning, David," Ruggerio began. "We had some further questions we wanted to ask you about the events on the morning your father died."

"Is my client under arrest?" Elkington said. "Have you read him his rights?"

Davis looked at the lawyer with that impassive stone face.

"No, councilor," he said. "This young man is not under arrest at this time. We are here this morning to continue our investigation into the murder of Preston Knox, and we believe young David here has some important information he can share with us."

Elkington nodded as if to say, *Continue*.

Ruggerio turned to look at David, who stared back at him. His face had lost color. His hands were tightly clenched and folded in his lap.

"David," Ruggerio said, "You previously told us that you came downstairs for breakfast that morning around seven a.m. Is that correct?"

Davie nodded.

"I will ask the witness to speak when he answers, as the recording cannot pick up nonverbal answers."

"Yeah," David said. "I came down sometime around seven, maybe a little later."

"And when you came downstairs, your father was there in the kitchen, is that correct?"

"Yeah," the boy said. "I mean, yes."

"What was your father doing when you came into the kitchen?"

David shrugged, his favorite form of communication. "I don't remember," he said. "Probably having coffee, reading the newspaper."

"Was he speaking on the telephone?"

"I don't remember," David said. "He probably was, since he spent most of his time talking to someone on the phone."

"You didn't overhear his conversation that morning when you walked into the kitchen?"

"I don't recall," he said. I glanced at Elkington and saw a glimpse of relief in his face. Obviously, the boy had been coached by his six-hundred-dollar-an-hour lawyer.

Jonah Allen flipped open a file folder he had brought into the room and placed in front of him on the table. He took out a sheet of paper.

"We obtained the telephone records of a woman named Camilla DeRosa," Jonah said. "These records show that Ms. DeRosa placed a twelve-minute call to the private cell phone of Preston Knox at approximately seven-fifteen that morning. According to your testimony, that would be the time you came downstairs for breakfast and entered the kitchen. Did you overhear your father talking to Ms. DeRosa?"

"I don't recall," he said. His face was now flushed, sweat beginning to form on his temples.

"Ms. DeRosa testified that she often spoke with your father during the campaign," Jonah said. "In fact, she has admitted that she and your father were having a sexual affair. Did you know about that?"

"No," he said.

"Ms. DeRosa has further testified that on that morning, when she was talking on the phone to your father, at the time you came downstairs for breakfast, she and your father were planning their next get-together. And, she told us, your father was engaging in, well, some intimate sexual conversation. Do you recall hearing that?"

Elkington tried to step in. "I don't see what this has to do …"

"We have a witness who says she and Mr. Knox were engaging in sex talk," Davis cut him off. "And that she heard someone enter the room, at which time Mr. Knox ended the call. Was that you, David? Did you come into the kitchen and overhear your father speaking with Ms. DeRosa?"

David Knox's head had dropped downwards on his chest. His face was now red and sweaty. He was in a box and he knew it.

He mumbled something. None of us could pick it up.

"Would you please repeat your answer for the microphones?" Jonah said.

"Yeah," he said, raising his head. His eyes looked wild, frightened. "Yeah, I heard what he was saying to her. Things he wanted to do to her body. How he needed to see her again."

"How did that make you feel, Davie?" I said. "Pretty crappy, I would think."

"Yeah," he said. "Pretty crappy. But it was nothing new. I knew he screwed anything that walked. He had been unfaithful to my Mom for years. That's why she went back to Boston. She'd had enough. She was going to leave him after the election."

"What did you do?" I asked. "When you heard him talking like that?"

"I was mad," he said, "Real mad. He hung up with that whore and I yelled at him. Told him he had ruined our family. Told him I hated him."

"What did your father say?"

David shrugged. "He told me to calm down," he said. "He told me he would always love Sam and me. He told me Mom understood, that she was okay with it."

"What did you do next?"

Davie shook his head. "I was furious. I turned and left. Went into the dining room. Where the fireplace is. He came after me, telling me to calm down. Said we could talk, work things out."

"And?"

His head dropped again. He mumbled. "I saw the poker. I picked it up and turned and hit him with it. It felt good. So I did it again. And again. He fell down, half in the kitchen, half in the dining room. He didn't move. There was a pool of blood under his head. It got bigger and bigger."

He stopped, tears now falling down his cheeks and dropping off onto his white dress shirt, causing gray spots to form and grow.

"What did you do then?"

His head came up and he looked at me, his eyes pleading.

"I went upstairs and got dressed and then ran for the bus," he said. "Went to school. Few hours later, the police from Barrington came, took me out of class and home."

"And you didn't tell them, or anyone else, what you had done?" I said. "Until now."

He nodded.

"Mr. Knox has nodded in agreement with the last statement," Ruggerio intoned for the recorders. "David Knox, we are charging you with first degree murder. You have the right to remain silent …" He went through the Miranda litany. David wept silently. Elkington put his hand on David's arm.

"My client will have nothing further to say at this point," he said.

"We have scheduled arraignment for ten o'clock tomorrow morning," Jonah said. "David, we'll hold you in a juvenile facility overnight, and the judge tomorrow will determine the schedule and logistics of what happens after that."

"Can I see my Mom?" he asked, voice wavering.

Jonah and I looked at Davis.

"Of course," Ruggerio said. "We'll give you a few minutes. I'll bring her in."

Elkington and David stayed seated. The three of us went out into the hall. Davis went down the hallway and brought Mrs. Knox back. I saw him whispering into her ear.

"No," she said. "No. No."

Davis held the interview room door open for her. She saw Elkington and her son and began to wail. It was a keening sound that came from someplace deep inside. Davis Ruggerio closed the door behind her and the sound disappeared. Except in all of our memories.

There was a press conference that afternoon in the auditorium at state police headquarters The place was packed. All the local TV stations were there, as well as the cable news channels, a couple of the networks and a dozen or more print reporters.

Colonel Wadsworth, resplendent in his fancy uniform, presided. Davis, Jonah and I sat along a table beside him.

"The Rhode Island State Police, after several weeks of diligent, professional police work in the case of the murder of former attorney general Preston Knox, has today announced the arrest of Mr. Knox's son, David l. Knox and has charged him with homicide in the first degree," the commandant said. "The motive for the killing was a private family matter. While we are glad to bring this case to a resolution, it is still a very sad moment for every Rhode Islander. A proud and distinctive family, already rocked by the death of its leader, has been further troubled in the resolution of this case. We trust that you all will respect the Knox family's wish for privacy and time to recover after these awful events."

The members of the press corps looked at each other, than sprang to their feet, yelling questions.

"What is this private family matter?" yelled the woman from CNN. "That's pretty vague. You've got to be hiding something!"

Wadsworth held up his hand.

"The suspect in this case is sixteen years old," he said. "Given his age, and the loss of his father that he recently suffered, we will withhold the full details of this case until it goes to court."

"When will that be?"

"The suspect will be arraigned tomorrow," he said. "After that, the disposition of the case will be determined by the judge assigned to the case. We will have nothing further to say."

There were a few more minutes of shouted questions and evasive answers. The state police had rung down the curtain on the case, and no matter how much the press squawked, they weren't getting any more information from our side.

One of the reporters from the Providence Journal came up to me afterwards, one on one.

"Chief Haddock," she said, "You were appointed to this case specially because the Governor appreciated your detecting skills. Did you work some magic on this case?"

I laughed. "Afraid not," I said. "Director Ruggerio of the Major Crimes bureau and Assistant Director Allen ran this case like the professional cops they are. I'd like to think I helped where I could, but all the credit goes to them and the fine team here at the state police."

That was mostly true. My lifelong opinion was that the state police's arrogance was often irritating, off-putting and undeserved. But, with the exception of Jonah Allen's attitude toward me, they had acting quite professionally in this investigation. Besides, the Governor had gotten me off the hook at the beginning of this case, which she didn't have to do, so I felt I owed her something.

"Why'd the kid off his dad?" she followed up.

I smiled at her. "Do you remember that quote from Tolstoy?" I said. "All happy families are alike, but each unhappy family is unhappy in its own way."

She did a double take. "Never thought I'd ever hear some small town cop from Little Penwick quoting Russian literature at me," she said.

I kept smiling. "You should come down and visit us," I said. "You might learn something."

CHAPTER 22

A COUPLE OF weeks later, on another Saturday afternoon, I drove Siggi back over to Deke Scanlon's cabin in the woods. It was now November and looked it. Most of the trees in the Scanlon Recreation Area had dropped their leaves and the woods looked cold and bare. There was a definite chill in the air that was not quite as bad as what the air felt like in January, but it was a preview of coming attractions.

I had called Deke a couple days earlier, so he knew we were coming, and so he wouldn't greet us with a couple rounds from his Remington shotgun. And I made sure to tell him that I was bringing Siggi, which I knew would be another defense against his impulse toward grumpiness. He didn't ask why we were coming, but I think he knew.

Old Dog was still in his place on his rug in front of Deke's crackling fireplace, and the view down and across Scanlon Pond was still pretty amazing. The water was the color of slate, which fit the mood of the day. And this time, Deke offered us some hot tea. I silently gave all the credit for that to Siggi's lovely presence. Even a professional grump can't stay mad for very long at someone like my Siggi.

We sat in front of the fireplace, sipped our tea and nibbled on the Oreos he had put on a plate. Old Dog raised his head in hopes of someone slipping him a piece of cookie. But when no one did, he thumped his tail twice, dropped his head and went back to sleep.

"So what is it this time?" Deke growled after a bit. I guess he was uncomfortable in a comfortable domestic situation.

"I've talked to the Land Trust," Siggi said. "Billy Church in particular. They've agreed to a special codicil for the land transfer contract."

"The what to the who?" Deke said. "I haven't agreed to anything, young lady."

"I know that, Mr. Scanlon," she said. "This is still a proposal for your agreement. But the Little Penwick Land Trust has agreed to provide eternal care and protection for the grave site."

"What grave site?" he grumbled.

"The one where Siobhan Scanlon is buried," she said. "And where, one day hopefully in the distant future, you will also be buried, next to your wife."

His eyes widened. "How in the tarnation did you find out about that?" he asked. "I didn't think anyone in town knew about that."

She smiled at him.

"It's pretty hard to keep secrets in a town as small as Little Penwick," she said. "A lot of people have forgotten that story, Deke, but there are still some who know and remember. And they all like the idea of you two united again in your own private space in the middle of the Scanlon woods. The land will be legally separated from the rest of the deal and made into what the zoning people call a special historic district. Under law, no one will ever touch the grave site. If you want, the Land Trust will construct a roofed loggia over the site and, if you agree, they will construct a special walkway providing access to those who wish to visit."

"Why would anyone in their right mind want to visit the graves of two old people who never did anything?" he asked.

"Oh, you and she did something, Mr. Scanlon," Siggi said, smiling at him. "You were in love, and that love has lasted more than sixty years. I think people will come from miles around to visit the grave of the star-crossed lovers who never got to fully enjoy their love. But for centuries to come, your final resting place will be a reminder to people not to give up, not to stop loving, not to let the nay-sayers and the haters win. It will be a memorial to romance and love."

Scanlon thought about that for a moment or two.

"Look," Siggi said, "I had the Trust architect do a rendering of what the site will look like." She handed him some pages containing architectural renderings of a round structure, just wide enough for two graves, with a low stone wall around the base, a series of white posts and a round roof covered in cedar shingle.

"They'll even install a plaque that will tell the story," she said. "You and I can work on the wording, if you like."

Deke Scanlon looked over the drawings. He didn't say anything, which I took as a good sign. Usually, the town grump was never shy of words of criticism and opposition.

"You did all this … for me?" he said, his voice a little husky.

"I thought it was important to tell your story," she said. "Your family did a lot for this town over the centuries. But you got the short end of that stick. I thought people should know. It would complete the Scanlon story here in Little Penwick."

Deke thought about that for another few moments. Then he tossed the drawings down on his cocktail table.

"I appreciate your efforts," he said finally. "I really do. But I'm going to have to think about this. I never wanted any fuss. I just wanted to die, get buried next to my wife and then the world could go on without me. That'd be fine with me."

I jumped in.

"Deke," I said. "You take all the time you want to think about this. No one is going to put any pressure on you, one way or the other. I will guarantee that. But if you want to accept this offer from the Land Trust, I think it could be pretty cool. A good way for people to remember Deke Scanlon and who he was."

He sat there for a moment or two. Old Dog stood up, shook himself, and then walked over to Deke and put his head down on Deke's lap. He scratched the dog's ears.

"I'm very appreciative," he said finally. "Let me think about it."

Siggi and I stood up and said our goodbyes. She walked over and gave him a hug. I'm not entirely sure, but I think he hugged her back.

WE WENT HOME. I started a cheerful little fire in the woodburning stove and looked for a college football game that would be semi-interesting to watch. Then I picked up Zinn's *People's History*, I had been pretty busy the last couple of weeks, so I hadn't made as much progress as I had hoped. He was now writing about the underclass in the pre-Revolution America and the men who joined the effort against the British for pay or to rise in stature in their society. He wrote about a man named William Scott of Peterborough, New Hampshire, who was asked to enlist for the Battle of Bunker Hill as a private. He offered to enlist only if he was given a Lieutenant's commission, which was granted. Scott figured if he was killed in battle, that would be the end. But if a few Captains above him got knocked off, he could get promoted! Scott was captured in that battle, escaped, fought with the army in New York, was captured again, escaped again by swimming across the Hudson River, returned to New Hampshire to raise his own regiment, including his two oldest sons, and watched one of them die of camp fever. He later saved eight people from drowning after their boat overturned in New York harbor, and died of a fever in 1796 while on a job surveying the new western territories with the army.

Just another ordinary American hero, I thought. *Sounds like a Swamp Yankee.*

I heard a car pull into the drive. Siggi got up from her knitting to look out the back kitchen window.

"Town police car," she reported.

I heard the sound of several car doors clunking shut and then there were people on the deck outside the back door. Siggi let them in.

LaToya Crenshaw came in, followed by Mattie Gonzales and his father, Hector. They were all smiles. Mattie came over and gave me a hug.

Siggi helped me get them all seated and provided them all with refreshments. LaToya and Hector had coffee, Mattie asked for a soda and Siggi and I drank some tea.

"What brings you all out on a chilly Saturday afternoon?" I said when we were all settled.

"I want to come say thank you for helping my family," Hector said in his halting English. "We thank you very much."

I smiled at the man. "You're welcome," I said, "But Patrolwoman Crenshaw did as much or more than I did. Still, I'm glad it all worked out."

Hector nodded. "My wife is getting some help right now," he said. "She is a good woman. But she has some mental things in her head." He touched his forehead to illustrate. "The doctors think she will get better. In some days. But better."

"That's great," I said. I turned to Mattie. "And what about you, young man?" I said. "No more cutting school for you?"

He smiled. "Nah," he said. "I told my teacher I would come every day from now on."

"Good," I said. "Although I will miss your visits to my backyard. Maybe you can come over on weekends instead. We can talk about desert islands. Or anything else."

He nodded. "I'd like that," he said.

"Congratulations on the Knox case," LaToya said. "It's all over the news."

"I try not to watch the news, much," I said. "Too much disinformation."

"They're calling you Rhode Island's most famous detective," she said with a grin. "The Pinkerton of Little Penwick."

"Which is why I don't pay attention to what they say," I said. "Disinformation and utter nonsense."

"Well," Siggi said, raising her tea cup in the air. "Here's to successful cases and happy endings."

We all raised our own glasses and mugs. To happy endings.

ABOUT THE AUTHOR

JAMES Y. BARTLETT is an award-winning American novelist who has published 16 novels after a long career as a prolific magazine writer and editor.

His epic historical novel *Year of the Sheep*, set in the Scottish Highlands during the Clearances, was shortlisted in the 2021 Fiction of the Year contest by BookLife, the independent publishing industry magazine from Publisher's Weekly.

He has also written popular novels set in the world of professional golf in his *Hacker Golf Mystery* series; and about small-town cops in the *Swamp Yankee Mystery* series. He has also published six nonfiction books in his career.

Bartlett lives in a small town in Rhode Island.

For more information about the author and his books, please visit his website at:

www.jamesybartlett.com

The Hacker Golf Mystery Series

DEATH IS A TWO-STROKE PENALTY
DEATH FROM THE LADIES TEE
DEATH AT THE MEMBER-GUEST
DEATH IN A GREEN JACKET
DEATH FROM THE CLARET JUG
AN OPEN CASE OF DEATH
P.G.A. SPELLS DEATH

The last four titles are collected in a box set e-book edition titled "THE MAJORS COLLECTION"

The Swamp Yankee Mystery Series

GLITTER GIRL
COLD SECRETS
RAINBOW'S END
FAMILY AFFAIRS
RUM ROW*

* *A Prequel/Novella available in e-book format only*

The Bach Musical Mystery Series

THE ORGAN JOB
THE COFFEE GARDEN
THE SONG OF ASAPH

Also available in German translation

Historical Fiction

YEAR OF THE SHEEP: A NOVEL OF THE
HIGHLAND CLEARANCES

Other titles by the author:

CADDIEWAMPUS: LOOPING FOR GOLF'S GREATS
SERPENT POINT: A POLITICAL THRILLER*
THINK LIKE A CADDIE/ PLAY LIKE A PRO
MASTERING GOLF'S TOUGHEST SHOTS

**Published under the pseudonym* Caleb Clarke

RUM ROW

A SWAMP YANKEE MYSTERY

PREQUEL NOVELLA

JAMES Y. BARTLETT

THE STORY BEGINS ...

It's 1924 and John Edward Haddock is facing a dilemma. He's been offered a freelance job: drive a boat out to Rum Row, where the suppliers of Rhode Island's bootleggers have a flotilla anchored just beyond the official boundary of the United States, pick up a load of illegal alcohol and bring it back to Narragansett Bay.

John Edward knows its wrong. And he knows the Mobsters making the offer are not the finest of citizens. But then, most of his fellow citizens seem to be breaking the laws of Prohibition with enthusiasm. And the money he's offered will help him start in on the construction of his dream home on the beach in Little Penwick. And, just maybe, he'll be able to ask for the hand of the lovely Vollie Jeffords.

RUM ROW is a novella that tells the story of this forebear of the Haddock family in Little Penwick.

READ THE FIRST CHAPTER

CHAPTER 1

John Edward Haddock was down in the engine room of his 35-foot cruiser, the Appian Way, up to his elbows in engine grease, diesel oil and bilge water, trying to get a recalcitrant nut to give way. He had already skinned his knuckles a few times in the small, dark space behind the water filters.

But he felt the soft footfall of a visitor stepping aboard through the starboard gate. Then he heard him.

"Yo! John Edward! You aboard?"

He grimaced down there in the dark hold. It was Chuckie Church, one of his oldest friends. John Edward and Chuckie had grown up together in Little Penwick, Rhode Island, attended the Boxford elementary school and Sunday School at the town's Congregational church together and had begun their high school studies when the world fell apart in Europe. Somebody assassinated Archduke Ferdinand and his wife Sophie, and soon all of Europe was engulfed in war.

John Edward, when he turned eighteen, had volunteered for the Merchant Marine; Chuckie for the Army. John Edward had begun, almost immediately, serving on transport ships running arms and materiel over to England, dodging the deadly German U-boats in the frigid North Atlantic, while Chuckie had taken the train down south to some North Carolina outpost until his unit, a year or more later, was finally sent 'Over There' to begin the march across France and Belgium with Pershing's Expeditionary Force, to push the Hun back where he came from.

The war had now been over for more than five years. John Edward was still involved in commercial shipping having worked his way up to the rank of First Mate, and everyone he worked with knew that it would not be long before he earned his commission as Captain. After almost ten years, he knew his way around boats, engines and shipping. He was disciplined, competent and mature beyond his 28 years.

Chuckie Church, on the other hand, was still bumbling his way through life, working as a truck driver, farm worker, lobster boat hand (he didn't do well at that, since he was affected by seasickness in the worst way), drugstore clerk, and now assistant manager of a grocery store up in Fall River. Everyone he worked with wondered how long it would be before he got fired. Again.

"Down here," J.E. yelled up from the hold. He heard Chuckie make his way across the deck, down the stairs to the salon before he leaned over the rectangular hatch in the floor which opened into the engine room.

"Hiya, Fish," Chuckie grinned down at him. "Whatcha doin'?" Chuckie was on the heavy side, with tousled brown hair and a crooked grin. He was wearing a flannel shirt under his leather GI jacket. It was December and the air was cold.

"Tryin' to change these filters," J.E. said, "And retain what's left of the skin on my knuckles."

"Thought you might want to join me for a wee drink," Chuckie said.

J.E. finally got that nut to let go and backed the bolt out of its hole. The filter came loose after a little back and forth shake. "Didn't you hear, Chuckie?" J.E. said as he worked. "They passed Prohibition. Five years ago. Booze is illegal."

Chuckie's grin widened. "Really?" he said. "Why, I had a few drinks just last night over at the Stone House Inn. Downstairs. You knock twice and say 'a guy sent me' when they answer. Nobody said nuthin' about Prohibition while they poured me a beer." He paused. "C'mon Fish. Life's too short to go through it dry. It's Friday afternoon. Should be a good group tonight. Maybe even that pretty little Vollie Jeffords will be there. Everyone knows you're sweet on her."

John Edward slipped the new filter into place, inserted the long bolt and tightened down the nut with his wrench. He nodded with satisfaction. Job done. Job done right. Knuckles saved. For the most part. He stood up, found a cloth and wiped his hands and arms clean, up to the elbows. He thought about Vollie Jeffords. Chucky was right. He had his eye on that one. The eldest daughter of old Harvey Jeffords, a lawyer in Little Penwick with a big house over in the Heights, where other rich people had big houses, she acted like she didn't know he existed. He saw her at church on Sundays and always made a point to try to speak to her after the services, but she was always distant, proper and cool towards him. Still, he didn't think she had a beau and was hopeful she might one day consider him for that role.

"Okay," Chuckie," J.E. said finally, "I'll go with you. But if we get arrested, I'll probably never speak to you again."

"That a threat or a promise?" Chuckie said and laughed. He waited while J.E. washed his face and hands in the small head, put on a new shirt and pair of somewhat clean and pressed trousers, threw on his leather jacket and placed his First Mate's cap, with the glossy brim, carefully on his head. He looked at himself in the mirror. He liked what he saw looking back. Haddock was tall and rangy, with broad shoulders, long arms and legs and a slender build. He had a square chin and deepset brown eyes that brimmed with intelligence. He adjusted the angle of his cap to what some would call a 'jaunty angle' and then nodded at Chuckie. "Let's go," he said.

It was a short walk from the harbor at Little Penwick, where J.E. docked his boat, to the Stone House Inn on the far shore of Round Pond. Off to the left, the open sea stretched out endlessly to the horizon. When they arrived, they ducked down a short flight of stairs at the rear of the three story inn and Chuckie knocked on the basement door. In a minute, the flap opened and someone's eye appeared, checking them out.

"I know a guy," Chuckie said.

"That was last week's password, you idiot," the eye said.

"Come on, Freddie," Chuckie said. "Let us in, for Pete's sake."

The flap closed, the door opened and the two young men walked in.

"So what's this week's password?" J.E. asked, curious.

"Let us in," said Freddie, who closed and locked the door behind them.

It was on the dark side in this basement room. There were two windows on the ocean side of the building, but it was now late afternoon in December, so there was no light coming in. There were two electric globes on either side of a long mahogany bar and each of the small tables scattered about, covered in red and white-checked table clothes, had a candle burning in the center, set in a little glass enclosure.

Despite the dimness, J.E. saw that the speakeasy was pretty full. There were mostly men standing along the long bar, dressed in jean jackets and canvas work pants, wearing heavy boots and woolen caps on their heads. J.E. knew most of them--they worked the waterfront here in Little Penwick, manning the fishing trawlers, lobster boats and deckhands helping with the ferries that came in daily from Newport and Providence, via Fall River.

The tables were filled with couples, and J.E. could see the golden light of the candles reflected on several women from the town he knew. The room had fallen silent when they walked in -- everyone was cautious and looked to make sure that neither Chuckie nor John Edward was going to arrest them-- but when they saw who had come in, they picked up their conversations where they had left off.

Chuckie went off to the bar, tended by Freddie, and came back with two schooners of beer.

"Canada's finest," he said, handing one to J.E. "We've had to drink this since they closed down the Narragansett plant. What I'd give for a 'Gansett right about now."

J.E. led them to an empty table in the back corner, but one still with a view of the fireplace crackling away happily. He sat down, took off his cap and sipped his beer. He had to admit, it tasted pretty good. John Edward was not aligned with either the wets or the drys, in fact, he tried to ignore politics as much as he could. He always said there were no Republicans or Democrats at sea, just men who were not yet dead. His job, as one of his first captains had told him years ago, was to try and keep it that way.

Chuckie was making the rounds around the room. He seemed to know everyone and was slapping men on the back, kissing the cheeks of the women, swapping tales and jokes with everyone. He's such a people person, John Edward thought to himself, as he watched his friend circulate. He should find some kind of work where he could just talk with people all the time. He'd be great at that.

A man was sitting at the far end of the bar, back to the door, where he could watch everyone in the room. He was dressed in dark clothes, still wearing a navy colored overcoat over black pants, and his hat was pulled down low over his eyes. He had seen Chuckie and J.E. come in, watched as Haddock took a table and Church wandered the room. He focused on J.E. and eventually, picked up his glass of whiskey --you had three choices in the speakeasy of the Stone House Inn: whiskey, gin or beer -- walked across the dark room and sat down at the table opposite John Edward.

"Mind if I join you?" the man asked.

"I think you just did," J.E. said.

The man stuck out his hand. "Max Frost" he said, by way of introduction.

John Edward ignored the hand and eventually the man withdrew it.

"I know who you are," J.E. said. "And I know who you work for."

Frost nodded, eyes locked on J.E.'s. "Good," he said. "We don't need no introductions or small talk then. Saves time."

Everyone knew Max Frost. He had grown up over in Westport, the first Massachusetts town across the border with Rhode Island, and had been working on the waterfront in New Bedford, just down the coast, when Prohibition had been adopted. Like a great many people who made their living on the sea, Frost had quickly realized that he could make a lot more money by running booze into the many small harbors, coves, inlets and rivers along the southeastern coast of New England. Outside the boundary of the United States -- the line had originally been three miles out; but Congress, realizing what was going on, had recently changed it to twelve miles -- there was a flotilla of ships full of European and Canadian booze. It was known by all as Rum Row. Smugglers like Max Frost ran small boats out to the flotilla beyond the bound-ary, filled their holds with as much booze as they could carry without sinking, and made their way back to the coast. They'd offload on beaches, in any of the small coves and inlets along the rugged coast, sometimes in ports, all while trying to evade the Coast Guard cutters and the local law trying to enforce the no-drinking laws. Almost since the moment Prohibition was enacted, there had been this cat-and-mouse game going on between the bootleggers and the law. So far, the bootleggers had been winning.

Frost was famous all along the coast from Newport on down to Cape Cod as one of the most daring and successful smugglers. But he wasn't the main man. Frost worked for Charles Solomon, known to one and all as 'King' Solomon. The King lived in Boston and controlled the flow of smuggled hootch up into Providence, Worcester and Boston. King Solomon was the local iteration of Al Capone in Chicago, Lucky Luciano in New York, Maxie 'Boo Boo' Hoff in Philly and the Purple Gang in Detroit. He controlled the flow of booze into the Northeast, paid off the cops, collected 'fees' from the speakeasies, and busted heads, or worse, for those who tried to oppose him.

"What can I do for you, Mr. Frost?" J.E. said now, his eyes never moving from Frost's face.

"You work for Columbia Shipping, amirite?" Frost asked. "First mate on the MS Gallagher, right?"

J.E. nodded.

"How come you're not working right now?"

J.E. smiled and raised his glass of beer. "Merry Christmas," he said. "My ship is in drydock down in Groton, getting her bottom scraped. The holidays is a good time to get that work done. We ship out again on January 9. It's looking to be a busy winter. Probably won't get home again until March or April."

"So you're at sixes and sevens then," Frost said.

"Not at all," John Edward said. "I'm working on my own boat. Always something that needs work on a boat."

"How'd you like a freelance job?" Frost asked. "Pretty good money."

J.E. stared at the man. "Thanks," he said finally. "But I'll decline the opportunity."

"Don't want to work for the likes of me?" Frost said, grinning at J.E. "Don't want to do anything illegal? Don't want to run the gauntlet of the Coasties who are patrolling the coast night and day?"

"Yes," John Edward said, simply. "All of the above. But thanks for the offer."

"You haven't heard my offer," Frost said. "I'll pay you one thousand dollars for driving a boat a total of 24 miles. I figure about six hours of your time. I don't know what that works out to, per mile or per hour, but you can figure it out. It's good money. And it's in cash."

John Edward's face remained impassive, but his mind was racing. A thousand bucks was about what he made as first mate ... for six months! If he had a cool grand in his pocket, he could buy that parcel of land he was thinking about above the beach and start building the house he'd been planning since the war ended. He might even have enough left over to buy a ring and ask for Vollie Jefford's hand. A thousand bucks! Life changing.

At the same time, he knew what he was being asked to do. Working in the marine industry, just talking with old tars ashore here in Little Penwick and over in Newport, he'd heard the tales and the gossip. John Edward knew about Rum Row, the flotilla of old wooden sailing boats and rusty freighters that was anchored somewhere out beyond the three-mile limit. He'd read how the sovereign limit of the States was going to be pushed out to twelve miles, come the first of the year. And he knew that bootleggers like Max Frost made regular visits out to Rum Row to bring back cases of illegal hootch to sell to thirsty throats all over New England. The trip out was not the problem, as long as the weather held. It was the one coming back. The Coast Guard had its cutters everywhere up and down the Massachusetts, Connecticut and Rhode Island coastline, looking for bootleggers. Night and day. And the cops and revenue agents on shore, if they hadn't been paid off by King Solomon, were another potential problem.

Still ... *a thousand bucks*!

Chuckie Church slipped into an empty seat at the table. His face was flushed from the effort of talking to nearly everyone in the place. His glass of beer was nearly empty.

"J.E." he said, "Sally Anderson over there said your Vollie may show up tonight, if she can put the slip on her old man. Thought you might want to know." He cocked his head and looked at Max Frost. "Aren't you ..."

"Yes he is," J.E. interrupted, "And Mister Frost is just leaving."

Max Frost stood and smiled down at them. "Think about it, Captain Haddock," he said. "But I need to know your answer by Monday. New Year's Eve is coming up fast, and our customers will want their orders filled."

He walked back to the bar.

"Answer on what, J.E.?" Chuckie said. "And why are you even talking to one of the most notorious rum runners on the southeast coast?"

"Never you mind," John Edward said. "It's nothing of importance. What time does Sally think Miss Jeffords might arrive?"

But even as he and Chuckie hatched their plans for the evening, John Edward Haddock's mind was still racing. *A thousand bucks*!

This Prequel to the Swamp Yankee Mystery series is available at Amazon.com, only in e-book format.

The other titles in the series:

GLITTER GIRL

COLD SECRETS

RAINBOW'S END

FAMILY AFFAIRS

are available in trade paperback, E-book and audio book formats. You can find these books, and others by James Y. Bartlett, exclusively at amazon.com.

Thank you for reading!

Thank you!

Yeoman House Books

www.ingramcontent.com/pod-product-compliance
Lightning Source LLC
Chambersburg PA
CBHW040525170726
48295CB00012B/346